STEVE

AND HIS S

Library of Congress control number – 201317037.

ISBN – 13: 978-1490521169

ISBN – 10: 14052116X.

For more information visit – www.stevesecrets.com

Email – softfocustelefilms@yahoo.co.in

To You, my Readers.

ACKNOWLEDGEMENT

Someone asked me to describe my feelings after completing my first novel. I expressed it in one word: Gratitude.

I am eternally grateful to God for blessing me with this wondrous experience of human life. My early life started with the grace, love and blessings of my grandfather, Akshay Kumar Bhattacharya, his elder brother Amarnath Bhattacharya and his wife Arti Bhattacharya. These three people have had an indelible impression on my life. Saying "Thank you" to these wonderful souls is not enough.

How do I thank Baba and Ma, my beloved parents who gave me not only this beautiful gift of Life, but also the gift to dream big and realize it? I am what I am today, because of the foundation they laid for me, with love and care. My childhood has shaped my existence. An integral part of my childhood is my dear sister, Krishna and my dear brother, Ajoy. They have been with me through thick and thin. Not many are fortunate to get a childhood embraced in love, like we three have had.

Life offers challenges to all of us. I had my share. Under every circumstance, I have tried to do my best. But there have been several moments when I found things getting a bit too difficult to deal with, all by myself. These were moments when a silent support has got me going. Little did I realize how strong was that support, how important was this person. This one person who stood by me in every situation, who prodded me along to complete this novel, against all odds, is my life partner, my dear wife. I can't thank you enough, Mona.

In these times of audio-visual media attack, the habit of reading is dying off. There is lack of good literature for children in our country. I remember how incomplete I used to feel when I had to tell the same old bed time stories to my son Kumar, when he was growing up. In a way, this novel is an outcome of that shortcoming. Kumar is in his early twenties now. Thank God that I completed this novel before he could say, "What is this childish stuff you have written, Baba?" And I would have had to reply, "Wait until you get married and have kids, son!"

This novel could not be complete without the support of some of my very caring colleagues. I am indeed grateful to Julia Fatou, Rahela Padachira and Pinaki Ghosh for carefully editing my novel, to Krishna and Balram for their creative illustrations, and to Damon and Benjamin for their apt cover design and beautiful formatting of the inside pages of my novel. Dinesh, Disha, Raj and Kumar have efficiently helped me reach my viewers. My sincere thanks to my good friends Sharada Sunder and Tanuja Chandra for their valuable advice. I will be failing in my duty if I do not thank my teachers Mr. Basu Bhattacharya and Mr. Joginder Shelly, my mentors, Mr. Subhash Chandra, Mr. Siddharth Kak, and friends Ashvini Yardi and Ashish Golwalkar for their constant support in my career. I shall always remember the help my uncle and aunt Arun and Purobi Bhattacharya extended in promoting my work. My humble thanks to them. In my early days of struggle, three friends came forward with unconditional help, Prakash Raghuvanshi, Sanjiv Saran and Rajiv Agarwal. I shall always remain indebted to them.

My readers may find this strange but my heart is filled with affection for the unconditional love and support given to me by my pet Sheena, who unfailingly sat beside me sharing every single moment of writing this novel. Only a pet lover can understand what our pets mean to us.

The great people who turned around my life and gave a meaning to it are revered Shri Devidas Hirode, dear Prasad Karmarkar, Swamy Ramkripalji, Shashank Gupta and Sneha Shah. I shall be ever so grateful to them.

My personal and professional life has been touched by so many wonderful people, friends, relatives, great books, and memorable films that have helped me reach where I am today. Though I may not be able to remember and recount every one individually, I would like to thank each one of them most sincerely for supporting me in their own way to complete my most prized possession, this novel: 'Steve Brown and his Seven Secrets.'

Last, but not the least, the first reader who read my novel. I will never forget the phone call when Vinodini Sunder, on the other end said, "Uncle, I could not keep your book down until I finished it. I read it in one go." Her words meant a lot to me. Thank you, my dear.

Any creative writing is of no use unless someone picks it up and reads it. I thank all my readers for finding my novel worthy of reading.

Table of Contents

CHAPTER – 1

AN INCREDIBLE CHRISTMAS

You are unique!

Do you know that you have the power to do or get anything on this planet?

Difficult to believe?

Steve Brown did not believe this either, until his life turned upside down one day. And the events that followed revealed a new Steve to him. Here's how…

Steve was lonely that night. He stood near a tall Christmas tree, hoping to shelter himself from the heavy snow and biting cold. Looking up at the festoons and tiny bulbs that peeped and flickered from under the snow that covered the tree, he fell silent. The glittering lights that illuminated the stores, the laughter of kids that filled the air, the tingling music that surrounded him, the bright festivities and fun…all this did not make much of a difference to the nine-year-old, who was lonely, hungry, and cold that night. How does it feel to be all alone in this world? No parents to snuggle up to. No relatives to talk to. Not even a home to go back to. Christmas meant a quiet dinner with a handful of friends in an orphanage, where laughing or even talking aloud was restricted. So, Steve preferred to be all by himself, out in the open, sharing the festivities of passersby. Now that it was snowing, the best he could was to go under the Christmas tree and brave the cold.

As he drew closer to the tree, something unexpected happened. A bright glare from a crack in its trunk caught his attention. He peeped into the crack and was shocked to see that the inside of the tree was in flames. This was incredible. In this cold winter night, how could a fire burn inside a Christmas tree, with no signs of fire outside it? In disbelief he put his palm on the trunk. The heat was so overpowering that he soon withdrew his hand. He wondered whether he ought to run away. But before he could decide, the crack grew bigger, the earth shook like an earthquake, and with a blast the tree caught fire. The heavy snow on the tree melted and gushed down like a waterfall, drenching him. Shaken and shocked, wet and shivering with cold, Steve ran for his life. After running blindly for a while, he stopped and looked around in disbelief.

Was this New York, the city that was bustling with Christmas crowds and festivities just a while ago? Before his eyes were desolate roads and empty skyscrapers. Not a soul around. Not a sound. The only thing that seemed animated amidst the dead objects was the Christmas tree, burning at a distance. Steve had no clue what to do next.

Standing under the snowing sky, perspiring with fear, he looked blankly at the burning tree.

But the worst was not yet over. As Steve stood frozen in shock and despair, wondering what to do next, the burning tree started moving toward him. It grew bigger as it moved, engulfing everything around it in fire. The tall skyscrapers went up in flames, the abandoned vehicles blackened and burned. Steve was dumbfounded. His mind had stopped working. All he wanted in this moment of havoc was to disappear from the scene. But by then everything around him was in flames. He had nowhere to go. Within moments, the towering inferno started to collapse, and with an earth-shattering blast everything came down. Steve shut his eyes with all his might, and the world around him blacked out...

This was not the first time that Steve had undergone such a traumatic nightmare. His own life was even worse than the worst dream.

CHAPTER – 2

A JOURNEY BEGINS

A distant sound of chants echoed in his ears. Still weary, Steve strained to open his eyes. When had he fallen asleep? He could not remember. Where was he now? He looked around and found himself cramped in a corner of what looked like the dark interior of a truck. There were about fifty other boys huddled together in the cold little space. He could hardly see their faces in that darkness; but from what he could see, they appeared to be from different parts of the world. Most of them were sleeping. Many must have traveled longer than what he had, he thought.

The mystical chants continued at a distance, punctuated by the reverberating sound of a gong. Steve could not decipher the language or the religious association of the chants. All he could guess, from the sound, was that there was a large group of men, chanting in some enclosed space. The chants made no sense to him. But they filled him with beautiful calm, even in that miserable state.

But the calm was soon overtaken by the cramps in his stomach. There was still no sign of food. In the last twenty-four hours, all he had had for food was a bowl of porridge and a dry bun. But he was used to surviving on little food, after all those years in the 'Holy Family orphanage'.

The orphanage building, in the dingy corner of a narrow lane, in New York, could have easily passed for a haunted house. Steve had learned to face the hardships in the confines of the damp walls of the orphanage. The room that he shared with eight other boys had just about enough space for each of them to spread a mattress and a hard pillow on the floor. When it rained, though, the space would get even smaller, because the leaking ceiling would not leave enough dry floors for all of them to sleep together.

At a tender age, life had been a big challenge for Steve. In moments of loneliness he would imagine how life could be with parents around. He didn't know how it felt to cuddle up to his mother or take a piggyback ride on his father. This void always showed on him. His cute face had a pair of glistening emerald green eyes. But those beautiful eyes were filled with sadness and suppressed anger. The long golden hair that fell on his forehead was often carelessly combed. He was tall for his age, but lack of healthy food had made him lanky.

Inside the truck, as Steve curled tighter, digging his head into his knees, he thought of the orphanage room again. This was the exact position in which he would sleep in the winters, when the damp walls would feel like the interior of a cold storage freezer. Although the half-inch mattress was hardly a shield, this curled-up position, in four layers of donated clothes, made it a bit easier to brave the chilled floor.

Enduring that cold was probably easier than braving the pangs of hunger, which were becoming unbearable now. That's when Steve remembered something and searched his bag. The tips of his fingers, peeping out of his torn gloves, were too numb to work easily. After some effort, he finally felt that familiar rough surface. Something he had almost forgotten about—that sweet bun!

An extra bun was a rare and eagerly awaited addition to Steve's always meager diet at the orphanage. And this piece of dry bun was especially precious. After all, this bun was baked on a day that was to change the course of his life.

That day had not seemed too special at first. It was just another day of working in the bakery—endlessly baking buns, just so that he could get his share of dinner that evening. His good friend David, a nine-year-old like Steve, worked with him at the oven, while the other boys worked at kneading the dough, shaping the buns, decorating, and packing them. It was Christmas time and the work had doubled. David and Steve were thankful that the heat of the furnace helped to beat the biting December cold.

Although they used to bake hundreds every day, Steve and the other boys in the bakery almost never got to taste those fluffy, dry fruit buns. David could not stop himself this time, and whispered to Steve, "Hey, Steve! This Christmas the buns will taste extra yummy, won't they?"

"How would I know?" said Steve. "We're here to *bake* buns, not *taste* them."

"Why not take one?" This was John, who was new to the bakery.

David smirked in reply, "Okay, go ahead."

John picked up one and was about to put it almost

entirely into his mouth when Steve jumped in and snatched it away. "Have you lost it?"

"What's the fuss about?" retorted an almost angry John.

Placing the bun aside, Steve whispered to John, "Don't you know Mr. Arnold?"

Mr. Arnold was the chief warden of the Holy Family orphanage. His wife had died while delivering a stillborn child. Since then, all children filled him with the dreary despair of death. Unfortunately, for him as well as the children, he was stuck with the job at the orphanage. And this had only worsened his bitterness toward children. He could see only one way out of his hatred for them—to whip it all out, quite literally.

Steve was warning John about Mr. Arnold's temper when he heard David scream, "Steve, the oven!"

Steve turned with fear; he had forgotten all about the buns that he had put into the oven. He froze as he saw the thick smoke wriggling out of the closed oven. He leaped toward the oven and scampered to open the lid. All the children looked on in horror as black smoke filled the room. Steve hurriedly took out the tray from the oven and squirmed as he saw it—a tray of two-dozen charcoaled buns! Not a word was spoken for a few minutes.

The smoke soon became unbearable. Choking and coughing, the children ran to the door. But before they could take in any smoke-free air, their breaths were taken away by the sight in front of them.

It was the lean and looming figure of Mr. Arnold, standing at the entrance to the bakery! The unshaven face of this forty-seven-year-old was partially covered with locks of salt-and-pepper hair, deliberately combed across the top of his head to hide an errant bald patch above the forehead and tied into an inch-long ponytail. But his baldness continued to defy him; at the back of his head it peaked through the tightly combed, greased-up hair. The long, bushy hair on his ear, seen even from behind, seemed to compensate for the thinning hair on his head.

His right eye was partially covered with his hair, but his other eye could look through anyone from within its dark circles and bushy eyebrows. The heavy pouch, prominent under this eye, was acquired through years of compulsive drinking. The final accessory on this formidable face was a cheap cigar dangling from the corner of his lips.

That face, protruding above a droopy set of shoulders, was the theme of many a nightmare at the orphanage. And that day looked like yet another of those days that were nightmares to live through. This was the first day that John, who was standing ahead of the others, got a glimpse of that face, and he prayed that he would never see it again.

Steve, David, and the other kids stood still, uncertain about Mr. Arnold's next move. There was an uneasy silence as the black smoke gradually settled down, allowing Mr. Arnold to look at every boy standing there. Urgent, heavy puffs shot out of his lips from both sides of the cigar. Having scanned the rest of the boys, his eyes stopped at the new face standing right across from him.

Mr. Arnold walked slowly toward John. Stooping over the boy, he blew a strong puff of smoke at that trembling face. John looked up through the smoke to see those piercing eyes and fuming nostrils. He felt like he would choke on that pungent smoke. Involuntarily, he coughed, covering his burning eyes with his palm. Tears rolled down and

John rubbed his eyes, hoping that the burning sensation would stop.

Mr. Arnold grabbed him by the shoulders and shook him vigorously. Through all the shaking, John heard a hoarse voice screaming, "Oh stop, you! Stop coughing and putting on this weepy act of yours! So we have yet another sissy in our midst. And what's the name of this one? You… *you*, I'm asking *you*!" Then, shouting louder "What…is… your…name?"

By this time, John had lost his voice. He tried hard but could not speak. Mr. Arnold had a way of leaving an indelible first impression—an impression that penetrated deep into a boy's vulnerable soul and stayed there for the rest of his life. John was no exception. He stood there dumbfound, shivering under the suffocating clutches of Mr. Arnold, who was still not done with him.

"That's it, you dumb nitwit!" And out came the cane, with a swish of its leather tip. An encounter with Mr. Arnold was incomplete without a meeting with this faithful accomplice, which he kept tucked beneath his belt—always by his side, like a sword.

Before John could register the full meaning of the sound of the cane, the roar from the smoke-filled mouth continued. "Out with your name! And the name of the ruffian who created this mess in my bakery!"

John was too terrified to do or say anything. "Listen, you…you wooden dodo! If you do not open your trap in the next few seconds, the rest of the talking will be done by my whip."

Saying this, he poked the leather tip of the cane into John's face. John had completely frozen by now. The only movement in his body was that of the tears that rolled down his cheek.

"Fine! You stubborn little fellow. Your countdown begins NOW! Ten...Nine...Eight...Seven—I just want your name. It shouldn't be that hard! Six...Five...Four—Speak up! Three...Two—This is your last chance!"

It was pin-drop silent. Mr. Arnold tightened his grip on his cane. The boys looked at one another in distress, praying that John would open his mouth. But he stood motionless as the final number rumbled out—"One! That's it!"

Mr. Arnold raised his stick and John shut his eyes tightly. He was about to strike when a loud voice uttered, "John!" Mr. Arnold stopped and looked around to see who had dared to open his mouth.

"His name is John," said Steve, loud and clear.

"Ah-ha! Of course, it's you, Steve—the leader of the gang," said Mr. Arnold, lowering his cane. "So here's the self-appointed spokesperson for Mr. John. Will you please step forward, Mr. Defense Lawyer?"

Steve calmly went up and stood beside John. There was an uneasy silence as Mr. Arnold wiped his cane on his pants and reverently tucked it back under his belt.

Steve knew what to expect next. Mr. Arnold grabbed him by his collar and pulled him forward. He leaned over and brought his face uncomfortably close to Steve's. Clutching his cigar with the corner of his lips, he spoke in a threateningly loud, husky whisper. "So. What exactly is wrong with your friend? Has Mr. John lost his tongue? Have his tonsils fallen off his vocal chords?"

Steve hated the way this man spoke, but replied calmly, "Mr. Arnold...John is—"

"Did I hear 'Mister,' again? You continue to defy me, when I have made it mighty clear that I should be called 'Sir.' I am not any 'mister' that you wicked boys can mess around with. Call me 'Sir'...

S – I – R...'Sir.' Do you understand?"

"Ok, 'Sir,'" said Steve. As if you've been knighted by some king! He thought to himself. "Sir, John is new. He doesn't speak much, not even to us. I think he got a little nervous around you. So—"

"So?" snapped Mr. Arnold, "Am I some kind of beast whose presence should make this poor kitten nervous?"

"Yes, of course! You are the biggest beast around." That's exactly what Steve wanted to say; but he decided it was better to be quiet.

"OK, now, let's come to the point. Which one of you is responsible for creating this mess around here?" said Mr. Arnold, looking around menacingly. "Come up quickly, admit your crime, and get ready for the punishment. Or else each one of you—"

"Me," interjected Steve.

"I guessed as much." Picking up a blackened bun from the floor, Mr. Arnold added, "Who else could be as creative as the gang leader himself?" He sniffed at the bun. "Mmm, what an aroma!" He brought the bun very close to Steve's nose and said, "Have you ever tried one of these special dry-fruit Christmas buns?"

"No, sir," was the short answer.

"So here is the chance of a lifetime. Go ahead: eat it!" said Mr. Arnold, mockingly.

"Sir, you know I can't eat this bun," replied Steve point blank.

Mr. Arnold's dark lips curled up into a crooked smile while one side continued to hold the cigar in place. "And why not?" he said, as he kept the bun pressed to Steve's lips.

Steve felt sickened by the bitter smell of the burned bun. Trying to free himself from the choking odor and strangling grip, he managed to mumble, "Sir, they're burned."

"Oh, are they?" shouted Mr. Arnold. "Oh yes, they are burned. Not just burned, they've been ruthlessly charred. And if a ruffian like you can't eat it, how can you expect anyone else to buy it? Twenty-four of these precious buns have been deliberately destroyed by this gang. You definitely don't deserve any dinner tonight. None of you!"

Mr. Arnold turned to walk away when Steve spoke again. "That's not fair, sir." The other boys caught their breath and stared in terror; what guts Steve had!

Mr. Arnold turned around, furiously puffing at his cigar. "What did I hear you say? What was that, you little scoundrel?"

"It's not fair, sir," was Steve's frank reply.

"Isn't it? So, what does your honor think is fair?" Mr. Arnold shot back.

Steve stood silently, looking at the vindictive man who hated him the most. A couple of months back, Steve had complained against Mr. Arnold to a trustee of the orphanage. The trustees had other, more profitable activities to manage and did not want to get too involved in the day-to-day workings of the orphanage. But they did reproach Mr. Arnold enough to rest their consciences for a while. Today was Mr. Arnold's much-awaited chance to avenge his pride. And he was not one to let an opportunity slip away.

He would surely teach that devil of a boy a golden lesson in obedience.

"Yes! Mr. Gang Leader," said Mr. Arnold, "what is 'fair'?"

"Sir, I am responsible for this. You can punish me, but not the others." Steve was soft, but firm.

"Fair enough!" shouted Mr. Arnold, with an evil glee peeping out of his eyes. "Fair enough, indeed! Boys, your gracious gang leader has decided to take all your sins upon him. This filthy head is going to bear the crown of thorns. Well, then…the punishment should fit this noble filth. Let's see…the punishment for destroying and wasting twenty-four valuable buns…what should it be?" Mr. Arnold looked around to note the frightened attention of every boy in his rooted audience. "Burning twenty-four buns… that definitely deserves twenty-four perfect strokes of my cane! And I'll give you a choice! Take all twenty-four on one hand, or make it easier and take twelve on each palm. Twenty-four strokes for twenty-four buns. That's fair, for sure!"

Some boys involuntarily let out muffled gasps. Until that day, "five strokes" was as much as any boy in that room had heard, or managed to bear. With renewed pride, Mr. Arnold took out his cane again and went on with a self-pleased chant of "Twenty-four for twenty-four, twenty-four for twenty-four…"

Steve remained silent. He quietly put forth both his palms. They were smeared with ash from the oven. Mr. Arnold looked at them with disgust. "Your palms are as filthy as you. Wash them well, after I'm done." Mr. Arnold turned to the boys. "Well, let's get started. Boys, you do the counting…one to twenty-four. Here goes!"

CHAPTER − 3

SHOCK OF A LIFETIME

The first stroke cracked on Steve's left palm—all of three inches long. He fell to the ground, writhing in pain.

"Come on, get up," shouted Mr. Arnold. "Or this will take ages. Now let's see your right palm."

Steve stood up slowly, wincing, and stretched out his right hand. Mr. Arnold raised his stick but stopped mid-air. It was weird. He clearly remembered whipping the left palm. But there in front of him it was the right palm that shone red. It was glowing, in fact.

"What kind of trick is this?" asked a bewildered Arnold. "Didn't I just hit your left palm? Are you trying to be smart again? Show me your left palm…Now!"

Steve stretched out his left hand alongside the right. Mr. Arnold could see the distinct purple abrasion left by the cane. Back to the right palm—It was still glowing red! A confounded Mr. Arnold was losing his cool. "Forget this. Let's not waste any more time on this stupidity. Get ready, boys. Here comes the second one! Say 'Twooooo!'"

Once again the cane was raised. With a fierce swish, it bore down on Steve's red palm. And then it happened.

Steve was still not certain what exactly followed. He remembered flashes of action and color. He remembered the cane coming down with a hiss and reaching his palm. But he did not remember it hitting him.

Those who watched have a vague memory of the cane landing on Steve's palm. What they remember clearly, however, is seeing Mr. Arnold flying across the room, as if struck by a thunderbolt. He hit the ceiling and came crashing down on a rack of buns. First the buns fell on him, then the racks, and, finally, the tins of dry fruits. And then 'sir' blacked out!

When Mr. Arnold opened his eyes, he found himself surrounded by the bewildered boys. As he staggered to his feet, he saw Steve standing away from the group. There, where he'd left him, Steve stood staring at his palms. As soon as he saw the boy and those wretched palms, he leaped up like he'd seen a ghost.

"Murderer!" he screamed, pointing at Steve. "He tried to murder me! He wanted to kill me!" Shouting like a madman, he pushed his way out of the group crowded around him. He continued to scream "Murderer!" as he ran out of the bakery.

Awe-struck eyes followed the screaming until he was out of sight. Then, as if in an orchestrated move, all heads turned to Steve. He was still rooted there, staring at his palms in disbelief.

The boys regrouped around the newest spectacle. The notorious right palm now looked normal. Not the slightest hint of the cane's impact. But the left palm was swollen, with a deep scar in the middle. How could one hand be so badly affected while the other remained stubbornly fine?

That night Steve burned in fever. The freezing floor made it worse. Shaken by the events of the day and the ceaseless pain in his left palm, he tossed without sleep. He wasn't given any dinner. The hunger made the shivering uncontrollable. He was trying to snuggle his head into his knees when he heard voices that seemed to come from the hall. It sounded like an argument, and the volume was steadily increasing.

Steve quietly walked out of the room, across the corridor, and toward the hall. The door of the hall was left slightly open, just enough for Steve to get a good peek into the room. He could clearly see the orphanage trustees gathered around a table. They were listening to someone, who seemed to be standing somewhere close to the door. Steve struggled to get a view of the speaker. It was Mr. Arnold, flaunting a bandage across his forehead and gesticulating wildly.

"Yes!" he went on. "Trust me; they've been conspiring for some time now. All the boys have been instigated. Their ears have been poisoned against me. To think that all this time, I gave up everything to care for them…and they were plotting to kill me! And this was the blessed day that they unleashed their well-planned plot. It was only the grace of God that saved me. After all, he knows I've been working for these kids for so long."

"And who do you think has been behind this plot? Surely, not one of the boys of this orphanage?" said one of the trustees.

"Of course, one of them! He is very much part of this orphanage," said Mr. Arnold dramatically.

"That's preposterous, Arnold. These are six – to nine-year-olds we're talking about," replied a member in disbelief.

"There's a lot that six – or eight-year-olds are capable of. It's all well for you to think every boy is innocent, just because he's young," continued Mr. Arnold, determined to drive home his point. "I'm the one who lives with these boys. I see violence, hidden, just waiting for a chance. I see how they can—"

"Okay, that's enough! Who, according to you, is this plotting murderer?" asked a restless trustee.

There was a sense of fear rising in Steve, who was witnessing this drama from the door.

"Steve Brown!" announced Mr. Arnold.

Although Steve had suspected what was coming, he could not quite believe what he was hearing.

"Steve? Wait. Is this all because he complained against you?" asked one trustee.

"Come again…Steve, who?" asked another.

"Steve Brown," answered a third trustee. "The boy, who said that this man ill-treats them, blows smoke in their faces, and what not. Come to think of it, Arnold, you do reek of smoke."

"I don't deny that I enjoy an occasional smoke. Who doesn't? And we've already been through this. We're talking about something more sinister here. This 'boy' tried to kill me. We're talking of someone who can do *this* to me." Arnold theatrically indicated his bandage. "Think of the influence he'd have on the other 'innocent' boys."

"Somehow I can't get myself to believe you," spoke one of the trustees.

"Don't you believe these scars all over my body? These

stitches on my forehead?" Mr. Arnold went on pointing out all his wounds. "Can this happen accidentally? A whole gang of boys, led by Steve, attacked me in the most cold-blooded fashion. This matter should be handled seriously and immediately."

"What do you suggest?" retorted an impatient listener.

"Well, we should do what is done in any other case of attempted murder. We should call the police."

Steve's heart sank, and he could not continue to look inside. As he lowered his head, he heard, "Have you lost your mind, Arnold? Police proceedings against a little kid?"

Another trustee continued, "And what about our reputation? Police entering these premises...it'll be shameful. We can't allow that."

Mr. Arnold was not one to be subdued like this. "In that case, I will have to resign." Firmly, he continued, "I have served the orphanage all my life. And I don't mind that you don't want to protect me. But the kids...they're my responsibility. I cannot stay here while I see a rotten apple spoiling them all. He's not meant for an orphanage. These sorts of boys need a good remand home. It'll be best for him!"

Steve felt like rushing in to tell the real story. He was about to push the door open when a hand stopped him from behind. It was John. John shook his head strongly, pleading him not to go in. Steve relented.

Inside the hall, there was a long spell of silence as the trustees stared at Mr. Arnold and then each other. Finally the chairman came up with a suggestion.

"Last month I received a letter from a Buddhist monastery, situated somewhere in Northern India, in the Himalayan mountains.

Apparently, they adopt orphans from all over the world, every year. They induct them into the monastery and bring them up as monks. I was not too sure about sending one of our boys so far away. We can't say how people will react if they come to know this. But, in this case, it might be best for all. And we will, of course, keep this among ourselves."

The chairman's suggestion was unanimously accepted. Mr. Arnold tried to hide a smile. Steve, behind the door, tried to hide a tear. For all these years, irrespective of the ill-treatment, or even the not so conducive conditions, the four walls of the orphanage were all that he knew in the name of shelter. The handfuls of friends were the only companions he had shared his life with. This was his world. To leave this and accept an alien world was the last thing he would ask for. But, sadly, he didn't have a choice. The decision had been taken.

It was early next morning when Steve was ready with a small handbag, stuffed with donated clothes. Most of the boys were sleeping and later would repent not bidding farewell to their dear friend. Only David and John were with him. As he walked out of the room, Steve turned to get a last glimpse of his roommates. He walked the length of the corridor with David and John and was about to open the main door when he heard a voice from behind.

"Steve! Come here, darling." This was Susan, the cook. The boys called this roly-poly middle-aged lady "Aunt Susie." She was the only source of real affection within the dank walls of the orphanage.

Susan took Steve to the kitchen and said, "I know you didn't do anything wrong. It's a dirty world in here. Maybe it's better for you to be going far away. I will always pray for you." She hugged him and took out a dry-fruit Christmas bun from the pocket of her apron.

"You have slogged all these days to bake hundreds of these, but never got to taste one. Here; keep this in your bag and eat it when you are hungry. Goodbye, my child." Susan turned away to hide her tears.

"Thank you, Aunt Susie," said Steve to himself, in the truck with the sleeping boys, as he looked at the somewhat dry bun that he had preserved in his bag. After that long and weary journey, nothing could be more welcome than this handmade Christmas bun. He took a big bite. Each munch filled him with bittersweet memories of the orphanage, his friends, and the events that he had left behind.

Then a knock at the steel door of the truck startled him. He could hear voices outside the truck. "Come on, wake up. Wake up, boys." The other boys in the truck started stirring, slowly rising from their slumber.

The door of the truck swung open. There was an explosion of golden light in the darkness of the truck as it was flooded by the bright morning sun. Along with the rays came in a light mist and a gentle but chilly breeze. The air was colder than any air Steve had ever experienced. The boys folded themselves tightly inside their jackets and jumped off the truck, one after another. Before he jumped, Steve peeped out of the truck. And there he stayed, captivated by what he saw!

CHAPTER – 4

FIRST GLIMPSE OF THE HIMALAYAS

Steve's eyes drank in the sight—the majestic range of the Himalayas, spread all around him! In the glow of the early morning rays, the snowcapped mountains shined like molten gold.

Just above the foothills, almost one with the mountains was the quaint structure of a Buddhist monastery. Tapering roofs of bright red and maroon rested on huge pillars and snow-white walls. And surrounding this beautiful structure were pine trees that spread for miles. These trees seemed to extend all the way into the clouds. And the leaves, they looked so fresh, as if they had just been sparkle-cleaned.

Now the chanting was clearer. What Steve had heard inside the truck was coming from the monastery in front of him. Steve imagined that there must be a large group of people inside a huge hall. His body was now resonating with the mesmerizing harmony. It was as if his pulse was moving with the rhythm of the chanting.

Mantra after mantra, emanating from the monastery, seemed to dissolve among the pine trees, rise up to the mountains, and return to him, soothing all the pain that he had ever experienced. Was this the house of God? Thought Steve, feeling gripped by some kind of love. Then, from the memories of his not-so-love-filled days, popped out a familiar image—that of the Holy Family orphanage and the concrete jungle of New York. These childhood impressions were so deep rooted, that Steve could not imagine that the world could be anything but harsh. And now before his eyes stood an all together different world. He looked forward to this different, if not better, life here.

Steve stood there, seized by the beauty of the sounds and sights, when someone touched his shoulder gently. At first he did not notice, because he was not used to a soft touch. When he was tapped again, he turned and saw a young monk smiling at him. Draped in a long maroon dress that looked like a gown, this gentle person with the shaved head looked very serene. He took Steve's hand and they started walking. Bewildered and somewhat scared, Steve looked around blankly, deep in thoughts. Thoughts of the incidents that happened so rapidly, that he had no time to take charge of himself. Engrossed in his thoughts he did not notice a stone and tripped over it. Thanks to the monk who had held him carefully, he did not fall. The monk noticed that Steve was embarrassed. He patted him and spoke softly, "What are you thinking?"

Steve was so deep in thought and yet his mind was blank. "Um...I'm thinking...of my home I have left behind. I was not happy there, but I was ok. It's ok to be sad, I suppose. Being sad made me comfortable. Here, I am not quite sad, but I am not comfortable, either. I am not used to not being sad. Actually, I am not sure if this is what I was thinking. I really don't know..."

"It's ok to be sad sometimes," said the monk, trying to understand Steve's mind, which was preoccupied with the struggles of his past. Wanting to comfort Steve, he added, "Life can be challenging at times and situations beyond your control can make you sad. But should you be sad always? Does sadness really make you comfortable? Some of us are so used to being sad, that happiness scares us. Sometimes, when we move out of our known surrounding into a new one, we are not able to accept it even if it is a better one. Our habitual thoughts keep us stuck to a situation. It stops us form embracing change. All we have to do is to start thinking differently. Think good thoughts and trust me, good things will happen to you. Come, let's move on..." said the monk, and he guided Steve toward the monastery.

The narrow pebbled path leading down to the monastery was lined with tall pine trees. The wind and mist that rustled through the leaves carried the fragrance of wild flowers. The bushes on the side of the pebbled path were bathed in dew drops, which glistened like pearls in the morning sun. Butterflies fluttered around, occasionally brushing against Steve. A few steps away, he noticed a tiny bird struggling to fly. Its weak wings were not yet ready to soar. The monk saw the bird, picked it up, and softly placed it in its nest on a low branch nearby.

By now they had reached the large courtyard in front of the monastery. The magnificent building looked even more impressive now. The tiled roof was lined with saffron flags that fluttered in a harmonious rhythm in the soft breeze.

Along the wall were large cylindrical metal structures. These brightly painted cylinders had scriptures of some kind inscribed in gold. A group of young monks walked past the cylinders, rolling them with a gentle touch. As the cylinders rolled, they produced a humming sound that echoed all over the valley.

The young monks made two rows on both sides of a huge door, which was closed. They lit a bunch of large incense sticks and waved them in the air. The whole atmosphere was filled with a mystical fragrance. Then the young monks started chanting. The humming of the cylinders, the chanting of the young monks, and the fragrance of the incense created an ambience of absolute peace. Steve felt one with the universe, spellbound by all that was happening around him.

Then a loud droning sound drew him out of his trance. He looked around and saw two groups of monks carrying two large trumpet-like musical instruments. The instruments were about six or seven feet long, broad at one end and tapered at the other, resembling the trunk of an elephant. Four monks carried each trumpet on their shoulders. One person, walking behind them, blew into it. The sound was long and hollow, and its vibrations seemed to tug somewhere deep at Steve's heart. All the groups of monks—the incense burners, the trumpet carriers, the chanters—formed rows along the pathway that led to the main door of the monastery building. The droning trumpets and the synchronized chanting grew louder, as if summoning the doors to open. They were all waiting for someone. Steve noticed that there were young monks, a few years older than him, who stood in two rows facing him and his companions. Draped in saffron gown like clothes, their heads shaven, these young monks looked calm and composed. Folding their hands, they bowed their head in respecting for the person whose arrival was keenly awaited.

Steve's eyes were fixed on the huge doors as he wondered who was about to emerge from within. The other boys who had traveled with him were getting impatient. Suddenly a big gong sounded and the majestic doors of the monastery opened slowly. Steve caught a glimpse of the interior of the monastery. He could see a wide and high-ceilinged hall, lit up with hundreds of lamps. As the doors opened wider, the lamps flickered with the wind. In the dancing lights, the dragons and other figures painted on the walls seemed to move. A long corridor stretched beyond the hall. At the end of the corridor, Steve could make out the figures of four monks moving toward the door. They were holding the ends of a large white cloth that was spread out like a movie screen. As the men moved closer, the cloth sparkled with flickering violet spots, as if the back of the cloth was lined with tiny lights like those adorning a Christmas tree.

At the door, the curtain was lowered, but there were no flickering violet lights. What appeared from behind was an old Buddhist monk, who seemed to have the kindest eyes and the most loving smile that Steve had ever seen. As soon as the old monk appeared, the sound of the trumpets and the chanting stopped. The silence in the courtyard was immediately taken over by the chirping of birds, as the old monk walked toward the boys.

Steve thought that there was something unusual about the walk. As he gazed down, he realized that the monk's feet were not touching the ground. He seemed to be floating a few inches above the earth. Like Steve, the other boys stared in disbelief. And for the first time since they got off the truck, they felt a little scared.

But as soon as the old monk spoke, every fear in every boy melted into a pure and quiet joy. "My beloved children, welcome to the abode of Love—the Gompa! In this house of God, there is no anger, there is no fear. Everyone is loved, everyone is dear. Today you enter a world devoid of hatred, jealousy, judgment, or violence. Here we are all children of God; we live and spread the message of Love. Welcome to God's land!"

The kind voice bathed the boys in love. Some of them, including Steve, could not hold back their tears. A monk standing next to him gently wiped Steve's face. A drop of tear glistened on the monk's finger like a gem in the rays of the morning sun. Showing Steve the sparkling tear, the monk said, "These are precious diamonds. From this moment, they will never flow out of pain. Preserve them and spread the message of Happiness and Love!"

Two monks lit incense sticks inside a perforated silver bowl. They then asked the boys to come and stand before the old monk, one at a time. For each boy, the old monk moved the incense bowl around his body, encircling him in white smoke. Later, Steve learned that this "smoke bathing" ritual was to purify the aura of the new boys. All this was mystifying and unbelievable for Steve. He observed the boys intently and noticed a marked change in their appearance. The moment the smoke bathing ritual was done, each boy's tired and sad face brightened up with a cheerful smile. This was unusual for Steve, who had not smiled in all these years. He was apprehensive of going through this ritual. In silence he kept observing the proceedings.

After the smoke ritual, a spoonful of fresh spring water was poured into the palm of the initiate. After sipping the water, the boy was taken into the monastery.

Steve was the last boy in the row. Reluctantly he walked up to the old monk and looked at his serene face. The aging face had something uncommon about it. Although the lines on the face seemed regular, those on his forehead looked peculiar. As the monk bent to bless him, Steve got a closer look. He saw that the lines on the monk's forehead were shaped like the stem of a blooming lotus, whose thousand petals were spread across his shaven head.

Steve looked at the exquisite silver, smoking bowl, marked with religious engravings and covered by a perforated silver lid. The smoke came out of small holes in the lid. It was tied to a delicate silver chain which was held by the old monk.

"Close your eyes," said the monk to Steve as he circled the bowl around Steve's head. Steve reverently shut his eyes, and the smoke encircled his body. Just then something happened, which was like a miracle of sorts. A simple ritual that all the boys had gone through turned out to be a sight to behold as Steve was being put through it.

There was a sigh of astonishment from everyone watching, as the white smoke turned violet around Steve's forehead. As the incense bowl was lowered along Steve's body, the smoke turned from violet to indigo to blue, green, yellow, orange, and red. Everyone watched this wonderful sight in complete silence. Steve's body seemed to have disappeared behind a mystical rainbow smoke screen.

The old monk closed his eyes and meditated in silence. After a few moments, as the thick rainbow smoke started to dissolve, he looked at Steve and spoke softly, "Open your eyes, Steve!"

Steve felt as if he had woken up from a deep slumber. How could the monk know his name? He looked bewildered, into the old monk's eyes. Those kind eyes had turned blue, as though they held the deep waters of the ocean.

"Steve, my child, I am Shom. For ages I have waited for you to come to me. Finally that day is here." He looked up into the sky. "Thank you, my Lord!"

Steve could not believe his ears. How could someone speak without opening his mouth? And he felt as if he had heard the voice not in his ear but in his heart. He kept looking at the monk, in complete admiration, as Shom took a spoonful of spring water and said, "Show me your right palm, Steve."

Steve suddenly remembered the incident when his right palm had strangely caused Mr. Arnold to streak across the room. That one unexplainable incident had changed the course of his life. He did not want anything of that sort to happen again. So he stood there silently without moving his hands.

"What is wrong, Steve?" asked Shom "What are you thinking? Have no fear. You will only be given some water to drink."

After a moment's hesitation Steve extended his left hand. At this, Shom was amused. He said, "My child, this is holy water. Ritual says that you should drink it from your right palm."

Steve rubbed his perspiring right palm on his trouser to clean it as much as he could. He had not forgotten the number of times he had been abused for having dirty palms.

Having rubbed it clean, Steve reluctantly produced his right palm. Shom uttered some holy words into the spring water and was about to put it into Steve's right palm, but he stopped. Steve followed Shom's shocked gaze.

Shom was staring at Steve's palm, which had started glowing. In the middle of the palm emerged seven curved lines bearing the seven colors of the rainbow. As Shom looked on at the play of rainbow colors, tears of joy rolled down his eyes. He bent down and kissed Steve's palm.

"You are the chosen one, my child! You will bring about the change this world is waiting for." Shom's voice was shaking with tender excitement as he hugged Steve.

Steve drank the holy water. It was water, but so sweet.

"You are holier than any holy water, my child" said Shom caressing Steve's matted hair. He then turned to the fellow monks and instructed, "The other can go and settle in their rooms." Saying this he turned to Steve, "Come with me." Shom held Steve's hand and took him to a pathway that meandered from the right of the monastery somewhere into the pine trees. The two continued to walk toward the woods, leaving behind a baffled group of young monks. None of them knew what Shom had seen; neither had they heard what he had said to Steve.

Shom led Steve through the pathway to a long staircase that ended in a garden lush with colors. As far as Steve's eyes could see, there were thousands of flower beds. A narrow path through the flower beds led to a small arch made of creepers. The arch seemed to lead into an enclosure of some kind. On top of the arch was a board made of flowers. This was an old plank of wood on which beautiful creepers had grown. On the creepers grew pretty flowers in a wonderful arrangement that read, "Butterfly Nest." Steve had never heard of butterflies building nests. He wondered how a butterfly nest would look if such a thing did exist.

He entered with Shom through a dimly lit passage. He could feel a soft breeze blowing from all directions, as if there were small fans fitted around the passage. Although it was rather dark, Steve could feel that the passage was abuzz with some kind of activity or motion.

As the passage ended, they entered a large space that was enveloped by a huge dome. It was the most colorful, beautiful, and incredible sight that Steve had ever seen. He soon realized that the dome was made of neither cement nor concrete, neither glass nor creepers, nor any other material. The entire span of the humongous dome was made by millions and millions of butterflies. The soft breeze that was blowing from all directions came from the fluttering of millions of butterfly wings. On the ground were beautiful plants made of tiny gems.

Shom guided Steve to the center of the dome, to a bench made of leaves. As they sat on the bench, it sunk like soft cushion. Shom watched Steve take in the wonder of the magical dome.

"Are you happy?" Shom broke the silence.

Steve was so awestruck that he did not hear Shom. He stared at the amazing kaleidoscopic dome, changing forms and shades every time the butterflies moved.

"Are these real butterflies?"

Shom smiled, "Why do you ask that?"

Steve kept looking up. "I never imagined there were so many butterflies in the world. And if there were, how could they all gather at one place?"

Shom looked at the little boy, full of love. "There are many more butterflies, in every corner of the world. But there are very few people who know about them. These butterflies are born here. You see these glittering gems on the grass? They are butterfly eggs that will turn into beautiful butterflies in a few days, and the Butterfly Nest will grow bigger."

"But butterflies always sit on flowers," said Steve. "I don't see any flowers up there. What are they holding on to?"

"You are right, Steve. There are no flowers anywhere in this dome. They are holding on to one another. Or, should I say, they are gently flying along, with one another."

"Why don't they fly away?" Steve was still perplexed.

"Like all of us, they are here on earth with a purpose. They are performing their duty of guarding a great secret. Today, no one in the world knows this secret, except a chosen few in our monastery. I am at one end of this secret. And at the other end, Steve, are you!"

Shom could sense that his words were confusing Steve. "Don't worry. You will understand soon. I brought you here so that you can make friends with these butterflies." He looked up and smilingly addressed the butterflies. "Friends," as he spoke, the butterflies started to flutter gently, "would you not like to welcome Steve?"

Soon a bunch of playful butterflies surrounded Steve. Some of them perched on his shoulder and hair. A tiny one sat on his nose! Steve was amused. "O my God, they understand your language! How come?"

"Every creature on our earth understands each other's language. It's only that we humans don't believe this. So, we are not able to communicate with them. You just have to connect with them with love and compassion and they start talking to you," said Shom as he could see that Steve was not able to comprehend what he was saying. He affectionately, he put his arm around Steve' and said, "You must be tired," said Shom. "Your friends will lead you to your room. Go, relax, mingle with your other friends, and enjoy yourself. Just remember, the Secret is not to be shared."

Shom bid Steve goodbye and fondly watched him follow the butterflies out of the dome.

The butterflies led Steve through the fragrant garden and the pine trees to the large courtyard where the initiation rituals had been performed. Then, for the first time, Steve entered the Gompa. As he walked into the outer hall, he noticed that there were no electric bulbs. Beautiful oil lamps illuminated the entire space with a gentle yellow light. The walls and the roof were painted in bright colors with figures of humans and animals, flowers and foliage, birds and dragons. The roof was supported by four strong pillars. Buddhist scriptures were etched in gold on these pillars.

In front of Steve, a large part of the wall was covered by two huge curtains made of white cloth. It looked like the cloth was covering or hiding something. Steve wondered what.

He looked around. There was no one in the hall. He slowly walked toward the wall. In front of the white curtain was a small marble stand carrying a marble lotus, whose petals were closed. When he reached the lotus, Steve thought he heard a gurgling sound, as if a fountain was flowing inside the lotus. Standing alone in the middle of the huge mystical hall, with larger-than-life paintings that seemed to come alive, a mysterious gurgling sound coming from inside a lotus made of marble, huge white curtains hiding something, and not a soul around—Steve was a bit scared and confused. He did not know where to go, what to do next.

"What are you thinking?" A voice, though soft as a baby's, jolted him from his thoughts. He quickly retreated from the marble lotus and looked around to see where the voice came from. There was no one there.

CHAPTER – 5

THE 'TRUST WALK'

D on't be scared, Steve. We all love you here." The childlike voice was so soft and so close to him that Steve wondered why he could not see anyone.

Steve mustered some courage. "Who are you? And why are you hiding?"

"I am not hiding. Look carefully, I am very close to you." The voice almost whispered into his ear.

"If you're so close, why don't you show up? Are you invisible?" asked Steve, trying to scan every inch of that hall.

"No, I am very visible and very close to you. But you are looking away. I am not on the walls or the ceiling."

Steve was beginning to get irritated. He looked very carefully at the pillars, the curtains, and even the white marble lotus in front of him. There was no sign of anyone.

"This isn't fair," he said, "You're playing tricks with me. I give up."

"Why do you give up so easily? I am so close," said the voice, almost into his ear.

"But where on earth *are* you?!" said Steve, finally raising his voice.

"On your shoulder," was the short-and-sweet reply.

Steve looked to his left. There was no one. When he turned to his right, he was stunned to see a pink butterfly—which was actually smiling at him! Steve was taken aback. Seeing him react, the butterfly flew from his shoulder and fluttered in front of him. "Hi! I am Pinkoo! Master likes the pink color that I've been adorned with, so he calls me by this name. And you are Steve. Right?" said the butterfly.

"Yes! I am…But you…How…how can you speak?"

"Well, all butterflies speak. But not everyone can hear us. Only the monks in this monastery and God's chosen people." Then Pinkoo added, "Now we have to go into the Gompa. But before that, pay your respects to Lord Buddha."

"Lord Buddha? Where is he?" asked Steve.

"See that white lotus in front of you? Touch it with your forehead."

Steve touched his forehead on the marble lotus. As he lifted his face, he felt the petals moving. To his surprise, the marble lotus started opening, and soon it bloomed into a beautiful white lotus. At the center of the bloomed lotus, instead of pollen, was crystal-clear blue water. Steve gazed at his reflection in the water, which flowed like a spring. It was this flowing spring that created the soft gurgling sound.

Pinkoo flew and sat on a petal. "Now, put this water on your eyes." Steve dipped his finger in the water and applied it to his eyes. Hundreds of lamps all around the wall started burning, though no one had lit them. As he looked up, the white curtains moved to either side to reveal an imposing gold statue of Lord Buddha. Buddha looked like he was meditating, his legs folded in a yogic posture and his eyes closed. Steve bowed before this calm-inspiring statue.

Pinkoo signaled him with her wing and said, "Come with me." She flew toward a corner of the hall. Steve followed her. Pinkoo flew up and perched herself on a painted door on the wall. "Come up," said Pinkoo.

"How can I come up a wall? I can't fly like you," he said.

"I know you are not a butterfly," said Pinkoo. "But you can climb up. See those stairs?" She pointed to a painting of a spiral staircase on the wall. This staircase led to the painted door.

Poor Pinkoo, she thinks I can climb this painting, thought Steve. But there was no point arguing with a supernatural creature, so he touched his foot on the first step of the painting. The next moment, the still painting seemed to animate. The stairs in the painting started to twist and turn. Soon they took a solid form. Steve watched aghast as a spiral stair case made of wood and steel emerged out of the wall. In complete wonder, Steve climbed the steps and reached the door.

"Was that difficult?" asked Pinkoo. Steve was too awestruck to reply.

Pinkoo led him into a dormitory, where Steve saw the other boys who had traveled with him. It was a spacious and cozy room. Each boy had a comfortable bed and a small cupboard to himself. Steve was filled with happiness and gratitude to feel the comfort of the bed which belonged to him. He put his small belongings into the cupboard and lied down to relax. The tiredness of the journey and the intense activities of the day had taken a toll on him. Soon he fell asleep.

A soft tap on his shoulder woke him up. A young monk asked him to come over and have lunch. The boys were taken to a large hall, where everybody squatted on the floor to eat. Although the lunch was very different from what he had eaten before, it felt wholesome.

After lunch, Steve spent an hour getting acquainted with the boys. Talking to them Steve realized that they were all from orphanages all over the world. Here were a set of new acquaintances who will befriend him. Though he had left some old friends behind, he was in new company and there was lot more to look forward to.

After the boys had spent time with one another, an elderly monk walked in. He was second in command after grand master Shom. Smiling at the boys he said, "Hello, boys! I am Vyoma. Well, I see all smiling faces around me. Now that you are rested and relaxed, I have a proposal for you." The boys looked at each other wondering what to expect now.

Vyoma could guess their concern. "Don't worry, it's simple," he said with a twinkle in his eyes. "How about going for a trek?" Everyone jumped at the idea. In the meanwhile, a young man, who looked like an assistant, came up to Vyoma and whispered something to him. Vyoma nodded at him and turned to the boys.

"OK boys, you have half an hour to get ready. I will join you soon." Saying this he left in a hurry.

In a private chamber, grand master Shom sat alone, deeply studying an old book. The book was unusually big in size. Its cover made of wood, had strange engraved figures created with ancient scriptures. The wooden cover had a solid brass lock which was probably put to keep its content secret. Shom seemed to be immersed in the book, as if he was searching something unknown within its frail, age-old pages. The room was dimly lit with two large candles placed next to the book. The big mass of molten wax dripping from the candle was testimony to the long hours that Shom had spent in the room. The room appeared misty because of the smoke that had escaped from the burning candles. Everything around looked still, the books on the shelf, the paintings on the wall, the hour glass in which small grains of sand trickled stealthily, even the black owl perched on Shom's shoulder with its eyes closed appeared like a statue until it opened its eyes with a jerk and ruffled its feathers as Vyoma entered the room. He stood quietly, wondering whether he should speak to his grand master who was immersed in reading.

"Come Vyoma," said Shom, without looking up, as if he could feel Vyoma's presence. Vyoma walked up to him and sat on the other side of the book. Shom closed the book and with a long, silent pause, looked at him.

"After spending all these years together in this abode of God, we have finally come to a moment in history that is going to change not only our lives, but the very face of our earth," said Shom solemnly. "This is a time that was awaited for centuries, by several generations in our monastery. Right now, this might sound a bit farfetched to you. And when the time is right, I will share it with you and some of our trusted colleagues. All I can say now is that we have stumbled upon an incident that will soon create a chain of events destined to go into the history of, not only our monastery, but also the history of our earth. And this is happening because of the unexpected arrival of a soul that has taken birth for the highest purpose on earth. This destiny's child is a part of Gompa now."

Vyoma appeared confused by what he heard. He knew that Shom would never mince words. Deep thinking went into whatever his grand master said, but in all the years that he had spent in the Gompa, he had never heard Shom talk like this. He wished Shom would clear the mystery and make things easy for him. Hesitantly, he asked, "I am finding it a bit difficult to understand you, grandmaster. What kind of a historical incident are we expecting and who is that soul you are referring to? Is he one of us?"

"Yes he is one of us, one of the newest members of our monastery. I am talking about Steve Brown," said Shom.

"That youngster who was inducted yesterday?" asked Vyoma, trying to understand what was unusual about Steve.

"Yes, Steve," said Shom. "Steve might look a regular young boy, rather withdrawn and shy. But he himself is not aware of the immense power he is born with. He is the child of God who was awaited by our Gompa for centuries. Steve has taken birth to bring about the greatest change to humanity and the existence of our world as it is now. I will tell you more about him when the time is right. For the time being, just remember that Steve is very precious to us. I have a feeling that there could be evil forces looking out for him. Do not express this to Steve so that he continues to be the way he is, but take extreme care of him."

Both Vyoma and his grandmaster remained in silence for a while. Shom knew that his disciple will take time to understand what he had just heard. After a pause, Vyoma spoke, "Though I am able to partially comprehend what you say, all I know is that your wish is my command, grandmaster. Along with all our members, I will take care of Steve in every which way." Saying this he took Shom's leave and went to join the boys.

There was quite a commotion in the boy's room as Vyoma entered. Going on their first trek was quite a news for the youngsters. They talked nonstop making plans and sharing it with each other. Vyoma had expected to see this scene in the boy's room. However, his thoughts were focused on Steve. His eyes were searching for Steve, who stood in a corner, rather aloof, not able to participate in the excitement of the other boys. "Hey everybody," said Vyoma, to draw everyone's attention. "I see a lot of excitement around. Bright faces just waiting to take on the wonderful experience. So what are we waiting for? Let's get going".

The excited initiates started on their first trek through the picturesque Himalayas. They walked across fields and tiny brooks on their way. Everything about the trek was enchanting—the misty green of the Himalayan valley, the gurgling of the brooks, the slight chill in the air, and the sweet fragrance of flowers that accompanied the wind.

When they reached the foot of a hill, they were asked to halt for a while. There, a senior monk—the trek leader—announced some new instructions. "Now we begin the most interesting part of our trek. It is called the 'Trust Walk.' We need to trek to the top of this hill, where a surprise awaits all of you."

As the boys murmured to each other in excitement, the

monk interjected. "Wait, that's not all." To the new members of the monastery he said, "All of you will be blindfolded."

The tone of the murmuring shifted from excitement to surprise, with a tinge of fear. The monk pointed to the young monks, saying, "One of our young monks will accompany each one of you. But when you are blindfolded, you need to surrender yourself completely to your new companion. You need to put all your faith in him." Then, speaking to the little monks, he said, "For your part, you need to make sure that your partner is safe. So, is everyone ready for the Trust Walk?"

The boys were not certain, but the task sounded interesting. First, they had to choose their partners. In each pair, it was the experienced monk's duty to blindfold his partner with a piece of black cloth. Vyoma kept a watch at the proceedings from a distance.

A young Chinese monk, who seemed to be of almost the same age as Steve, walked up to him and said, "Hi, I am Cheeka. Can I be your partner?"

"Sure. My name is Steve." Steve immediately grew fond of Cheeka's smile; it started from his eyes, which wrinkled into narrow slits with the force of the smile. Cheeka seemed as excited as Steve to go on the trek, which was why Steve was surprised to hear what Cheeka said next.

"You know, Steve, I have been on this Trust Walk many times. And every time, it's a new experience." Cheeka moved his gaze from the top of the hill to Steve. "Are you ready?"

Steve was a bit nervous. "Yeah, sort of..."

"Don't worry. Have faith in me. I promise I will not let you down," said Cheeka with his signature smile.

Steve took a while before he responded. "OK. You can put on the blindfold now." Steve was about to close his eyes when an unusual sight caught his attention. He saw a bunch of bats hover above his head, in a strange rhythmic cycle. They seemed to be flying in swiftly changing formations. The movement of the bats was so quick that at times they appeared blurred, and at times they even disappeared before his eyes. The bats created a sharp noise, which was unlike any sound he had heard before. They were like high frequency sound waves piercing into his ears. There was something mysterious about the illusion created by the bats. Steve felt that each of these bats was taking turns to focus its attention on him. This was making him uncomfortable. He thought of calling for help, but before he could muster the courage, the bats suddenly grouped together, one behind the other in such a row that Steve could see only the first bat. The others were hidden, almost camouflaged behind it. Then all of a sudden, they darted towards Steve. As they came closer, their eyes grew larger and blood red in color. 'What is happening?' thought Steve, 'Why are these bats after my life?' Petrified, he sat on the ground, buried his head between his knees and shouted, "No...No...Go away...Leave me alone... Help...Someone please help"!

Everyone around was alarmed. Some boys along with the trek leader and Vyoma rushed to Steve. He squatted down with a thud, covered his head with his hands and shut his eyes tightly. Cold sweat appeared on his forehead as he sat there trembling. He was numb with fear till Vyoma tapped him on his forehead applying pressure with his thumb. This gave him instant energy but Steve was not prepared to open his eyes. "What happened Steve?" asked Vyoma, putting his arm around him.

"D – D – Did you see those bats?" asked Steve, still trembling. Vyoma looked around. So did the other boys. There was no trace of any bat.

"No, my dear, there are no bats here," said Vyoma, trying to understand Steve's mind. "In fact, bats have never been noticed in this region. They cannot survive in this cold."

"But I just saw them. Hoards of sinister bats preparing to attack me," Steve was not ready to believe Vyoma. "Look up, just above my head, a whole lot of bats hovering there." Steve pointed his finger towards the sky, but kept his eyes closed. He didn't want to see the horrifying creatures again.

Vyoma could feel the fright that had sunk deep into Steve's heart. He wanted to help Steve come out of the horror. Gently patting his shoulder he said. "There is nothing to fear, my dear. Open your eyes. We are a strong group behind you all the time. Just believe that no harm can ever come to you. None of us see any bats here. So forget it as a freak illusion and relax."

Steve was more composed by then. He looked around and up in the sky, trying to find a trace of those frightening creatures even at the farthest distance. But nothing was in sight. 'How can this be?' he said to himself. 'I am awake and in this broad daylight I could not possibly be dreaming'. But he did not want to cause further embarrassment to himself and concern to others. He got up and quietly said, "I am sorry, I caused such a commotion."

"Not at all, my dear", said Vyoma, "Sometimes at this

height lack of oxygen can create illusions. It's perfectly OK. Are you feeling fine now?"

"Yes, I suppose," said Steve with a doubt in his voice as he noticed something strange on his shoulder, but did not share it with anyone. He did not want any more undue attention. Giving him a big hug Vyoma said to the group, "So, boys are we all set to start our trust walk?"

"Yes", was the collective response.

"Great, so let's go..." with this pep talk Vyoma re-grouped the partners. Cheeka came up to Steve and cheered him up. "Hey, never mind Steve. There is a lot of fun ahead of us". Steve still appeared stumped. Cheeka sensed his state of mind and tried his best to lighten up the atmosphere. Steve did not want to carry the story further and spoil the game, but he knew all was not right. Otherwise where would the blood stain on his shoulder appear from?

"Hey partner," said Cheeka to draw Steve's attention once again. "Forget it, friend," he said. "Let's get on with our game." Putting the blindfold on Steve's eyes, Cheeka said, "You know something, Steve? They have not yet told you about an interesting part of this trek; on our way back, I will be blindfolded and you will guide me."

"Wow! Um, I'm not sure about how good a guide will I be," wondered Steve, not quite confident about himself.

"You'll be great." By now the blindfold was tied. "OK. Can you wait a minute, while I find out what else we need to take with us?"

"Sure, I'll be fine," replied Steve.

"Good luck, Steve!"

"Thanks," said Steve, but soon he realized that it wasn't Cheeka's voice.

"Wish me good luck, too," continued the other voice. Steve thought he recognized the voice, but how could it be here? He pulled down his blindfold and peeped from one eye to confirm his guess.

"You!" said Steve. "What are you doing here, Pinkoo?"

"Why?" asked Pinkoo. "Can't I go on a Trust Walk with you? Master asked me to accompany you wherever you go."

After introducing her to Cheeka, Steve said, "Pinkoo, if you're going on the Trust Walk, where's your blindfold?"

"Here." Pinkoo plucked a hair off Steve's head.

"Ouch!" whispered Steve. "What are you up to?"

"Just watch!" In all seriousness, Pinkoo took Steve's hair and tied it around her eyes. "Now I am ready. I am putting all my trust in you, partner. Blindfolded, I sit on your shoulder. I will go wherever you go."

"You're crazy," Steve said with a laugh.

"Are you boys ready?" the loud voice of the trek leader alerted everyone. "Good luck to you all! Enjoy the Trust Walk."

Steve pulled the blindfold back over his eyes. He held Cheeka's hand and started walking with his support. Lacking sight, he felt like his senses of sound and smell were getting sharper. He could hear the sounds of various birds and insects. He could hear his own footsteps and those of Cheeka and his other companions. He could even hear and feel the occasional flapping of Pinkoo's wings, close to his ear. He could feel Cheeka's hand holding him firmly.

Cheeka kept talking to him, telling him whether he should go right or left and whether he should take a long or a short step, depending on what was lying on the path ahead. Although Steve was listening carefully to what Cheeka said, he relied more on his own judgment. All his senses were alert and making sure that he was safe. His keen senses had always helped him fend for himself in the orphanage. He trusted himself more than Cheeka.

At a distance, he heard the gurgling sound of flowing water. "We are approaching a small brook," explained Cheeka. "From here on, our path is full of slippery pebbles. You need to walk cautiously." They reached the brook. "This brook is not too wide. The water in the middle is knee deep though. If we walk slowly, we'll be able to cross easily."

It was a bit colder near the brook, and Steve did not want to wet his shoes and socks. From what Cheeka said, he thought he could jump over the brook.

"I think I can jump over it," said Steve.

"No, Steve, it's risky."

Steve got impatient. He let go of Cheeka's hand, and while his panicked partner warned, "No, Steve, don't—", Steve jumped and fell into the middle of the brook. The water was shallow, but all his clothes were drenched.

As he staggered to his feet, Steve heard a voice chide him, kindly. "You have betrayed Cheeka's trust." It was the voice of his Master, Shom. "Why did you lose patience, my child? If you cannot surrender yourself to the friend who is holding your hand, how can you surrender to God, whom you do not see? And you forgot, my child, that someone else was totally surrendered to you."

"Pinkoo!" Steve suddenly remembered his innocent passenger. "Oh my God, where is Pinkoo?"

"I am here, sitting on your head," said Pinkoo's

voice. "Don't worry, I am fine. Thank God I am not wet, otherwise…"

Cheeka rushed to the middle of the brook and helped Steve up. "Are you okay, Steve?"

"Yeah. That was stupid of me. I'm really sorry," said a dejected Steve.

"Never mind," assured Cheeka. "We are partners. Let's move on!"

"Yeah! Let's go! Let's go!!" Steve heard an excited voice coming from the top of his head.

The rest of the trek seemed much lighter for Steve, who had now absolutely surrendered to Cheeka. What a sense of freedom it was to be guided by another person, not having to bother about the next step! Steve was only worried about his wet clothes, especially because he expected it to get colder as they climbed higher. But, surprisingly, as they approached the top of the hill, the air became warmer.

At the top, the new boys waited with bated breath for their blindfolds to come off. Steve could hear the sound of gushing water at a distance.

Finally, the trek leader announced, "Here we are, boys. I must say, each of you did exceedingly well in the Trust Walk. Now your partners will take off your blindfolds so that you can see the marvelous sight in front of you."

Cheeka slowly untied Steve's blindfold. As Steve's eyes adjusted to the light, he saw it—a waterfall. But this was not just another stream bouncing down a mountain. The entire waterfall was wrapped in a misty haze. It was like a heavenly group of millions of pristine water droplets, bouncing like tiny silver-white angels with glowing halos around their heads. It took some time for Steve to realize that the mist was caused by the hot vapor from the waterfall, which was spreading warmth around it.

"Isn't it beautiful, Steve?" said Cheeka.

Steve was so lost in the sight that he forgot to reply. Then he heard that familiar voice again. "I've taken off my blindfold, too." Pinkoo placed the hair that she had plucked back onto Steve's scalp. "Oh, my, my! Isn't this gorgeous?" retorted Pinkoo.

"So this is your first visit, too?" asked Steve.

"No, the hundred and twentieth visit," said Pinkoo casually. "But you know, every time I come here, I feel like it's the first time." Then, she added sadly, "Like all the times that I've come here, I can't go beyond this point. I can't wet my wings. I will play around while you have a dip."

Steve watched Pinkoo fly away, then he turned to Cheeka in gratitude. "How can I thank you, partner? You've given me the most memorable experience of my life." Steve hugged Cheeka.

The sun came out of the clouds and formed a beautiful rainbow across the waterfall. As Steve looked at the rainbow, a strange feeling overpowered him. It seemed to start from his right palm. He looked at it—it was glowing. A hot flash ran through his right hand and spread all over his body. Steve felt his temperature rising. Cheeka, who was holding Steve's hand, could feel the change in his body.

"Are you OK, Steve? You seem to have a fever."

Steve's eyes remained fixed on the rainbow. It appeared as if he was in a hypnotic spell. The colors of the rainbow seemed so overpowering that Steve could not see anything. Just the seven magical colors, they seemed to send a throbbing through his body. Steve's strange behavior was upsetting Cheeka. "Steve!" said Cheeka in a rather loud voice, shaking his hand so that he would come out of the strange spell, "Talk to me. What's wrong with you?" Steve was physically there, but he seemed to be in some other space. He stood there with his look fixed at the rainbow, as his whole body shook vigorously. In the mean time, as if by a stroke of good luck, the clouds covered the sun again and the rainbow disappeared. Steve was back to normal. He came out of the strange spell and looked around. Cheeka and the other boys were staring at him.

"What's wrong with you, Steve?" Cheeka asked again.

"Why? Nothing. I mean, I don't know," replied Steve, a bit confused. He was not happy calling for unnecessary attention.

"Maybe you caught a chill when you fell into the brook," said Cheeka.

"I don't think so. I'm fine," said Steve, trying to forget the incident. "Come on; let's go for a warm dip." After a moment or two in the warm water, they forgot all about what had happened.

In all those years, Steve had never had such a refreshing shower. The water was so warm that it took away all the fatigue from his body. "This waterfall comes from the snowcapped mountains. It should be freezing. How come it's so hot?" Steve asked Cheeka.

"Actually this waterfall originates from a natural spring," explained Cheeka. "The rich sulfur content and other minerals make the water hot and good for health."

After a rejuvenating bath and lots of fun and frolicking in the waterfall, the kids were ravishingly hungry. And the food the monks had brought was inviting, too. There were momos—a local delicacy made of steamed rice flour, stuffed with vegetables—plus stir fried potatoes and vegetables sprinkled with mild spices, all of it steaming hot from the hot case. For the sweet tooth, there were a variety of cakes – from cup cakes, fruit cakes to almond muffins and chocolate chip slices. And to wash it down there was a tall glass of butter tea. The food was plentiful and the children could take as many helpings as they wanted.

All of them attacked the food hungrily. But Steve sat quietly, looking at the spread. He had never seen so much food in his life. In fact, he did not know the taste of most of the dishes. Although the kids at the orphanage baked exotic cakes and pastries, those goodies were reserved for the trustees and of course, Mr. Arnold. To taste a slice of cake would mean stealing it. And that was too much of a risk. So Steve sat there wondering which dish to touch. That's when he heard Pinkoo's voice again.

"What are you thinking?"

"Oh! You startled me again!" said Steve. "How do you always manage to appear at the wrong time?"

"Or is it the right time?" Pinkoo knew that Steve needed her help.

"Yeah, maybe…you're somewhat right," said Steve, reluctantly. He was not used to being open about his feelings.

"When you are hungry, don't think. The food is for all of us. See, I've got my share." Pinkoo had managed to get a chocolate chip from the cake. She fluttered her wings against his hands and said, "What are you waiting for? Go for it!"

Steve left his dark past behind. The next moment he was gorging himself on the delicious food. Cheeka gave Steve an almond chocolate that he had made himself, at the monastery. Steve was assured that he was in the company of loving people and good times were ahead of him. His first day in the monastery had washed away all his pain.

Night fell. A beautiful moon peeped out beyond the window, and Steve's bed seemed to be bathed in moonlight. Steve was looking at the beautiful moon when he noticed bats, the same ones he had seen on the trek, hovering near his window. To see those black bats in the dead of the night was a frightful sight. Steve was too scared even to close the window. Just then an owl hooted and the bats suddenly disappeared. Steve was relieved.

Lying on his soft bed he looked at the calm moon and thanked God for all the happiness he had been granted. He thought of his companions and friends back home, at the orphanage. How he wished that they could be free of that hell hole and live a blissful life here. Thinking about their pain made him sad. He was also reminded of Christmas, which was not too far. Even though there was no great celebration for the boys at the orphanage, it was a day which they would wait for throughout the year. This year, maybe Christmas would come and go without a celebration for Steve. He missed all the friends who had comforted him in his lonely moments.

Steve was deep in these thoughts when he felt a soft touch on his shoulder. He turned and saw his Master smiling at him.

"So how was your day, Steve?" asked Shom.

"I have never been so happy, all my life," Steve replied. "So much has happened in just one day. The Butterfly Nest, the Trust Walk, and then the waterfall—more beautiful than anything I have ever imagined. But something happened there. Something I don't understand. It made me really confused and, I guess, uncomfortable, Master." Steve stopped. He was trying to recollect exactly how he felt when he saw the rainbow.

"What happened to you was perfectly normal," said Shom. "Go on."

"I was standing on top of the hill, with Cheeka and Pinkoo, watching the waterfall. Everything was fine, until I saw a rainbow in the middle of the waterfall. I felt like I was being sucked into the colors. Everything around me— the waterfall, the trees, my friends—everything in sight was getting lost into some darkness. The only thing left was the rainbow right in front of me. Nothing else seemed to exist. The rainbow seemed to grow bigger and brighter. Then my body started reacting to the colors. First my right palm felt hot, as if it was glowing from inside. The heat went up my right arm and spread very fast, all over my body. I felt like I had a high fever. But I didn't feel weak, like in a fever. I felt stronger and stronger, so powerful that I didn't know what to do next. I was scared. Then, thank God, the sun went behind the clouds. The rainbow disappeared, and within a few seconds everything was back to normal." As Steve narrated the incident, huge drops of perspiration appeared on his forehead and he breathed heavily.

Shom was sitting quietly beside Steve. He wiped the perspiration off Steve's forehead and hugged him. There was such magic in his Master's hug that Steve calmed down immediately.

"Steve, you are the most wonderful child of God. And trust me, whatever happened to you was absolutely normal.

For anyone else, it would have been alarming. But you are different from others. You are special, my child!" Shom said with his ever-loving smile. "Now. May I see your right hand?"

Steve showed his hand. Shom looked at it carefully. "Look at the lines of your right palm. These seven curved lines at the center of your palm form a rainbow. And this is not a coincidence. Watch carefully." Shom closed his eyes and silently uttered some mantras. After a few moments, he took a deep breath and blew gently on Steve's palm. And then...it happened! The seven lines on his palm started glowing with the seven colors of the rainbow. At first, Steve stared in disbelief. But gradually the glow of the rainbow became brighter and brighter, and Steve felt that he was getting sucked into it again. His body temperature started rising and he had that feeling of immense power. The glow was so strong that it illuminated the whole room. Steve's face was flushed, as though there was a spirit made of light growing inside him. Shom watched Steve and continued chanting. Finally, he closed Steve's palm and softly blew on his clenched fist. Slowly, the glow disappeared and Steve was back to normal. Steve loosened his fist and started breathing normally. Shom took Steve in his arms and caressed his hair.

"What is all this, Master?" Steve asked in his confusion. "Are you a magician?"

Shom smiled. "No, my son. This is not magic. It is real."

"But I don't understand any of this." Steve couldn't forget that feeling, that mystical experience. "I need help."

With an affectionate smile, Shom said, "Sometimes we do not understand the purpose for which God has sent us to this earth. Right now I can only say that this rainbow, with which you were born, is for the good of humanity. It will never harm you. You will realize its power very soon.

"Of course, you need to learn more about yourself and this world. Tomorrow we will meet before sunrise, at the Butterfly Nest. Someone will escort you there. It's getting late now. Sleep well, my child. Goodnight."

Saying this, Shom touched Steve's forehead with his thumb. It made Steve very calm and sleepy. He dozed off into a sound sleep as Shom left the room.

CHAPTER – 6

THE SECRET

"Good morning." A sweet, familiar voice woke Steve up from a pleasant sleep. He opened his eyes to see little Pinkoo sitting on his nose and smiling at him.

"Good morning, Pinkoo," murmured a sleepy Steve. "You always show up at the right place, at the right time."

"You are right," Pinkoo replied. "Now get ready quickly. You have a long day ahead."

Steve was looking forward to everything that was destined for him. He knew that in this house of God, anything that came to him would be a gift of the Lord. However, his old beliefs, fears and doubts had not left him. Years of living in pain had had an indelible impression on his personality. Accepting new situations was not easy for him. He was always under a low self esteem and realizing that he was special was unacceptable for him.

However, a forced sense of discipline imposed at the orphanage, always followed him. In no time he was bathed and dressed. Pinkoo took him to the main hall of the Gompa. The whole place was filled with the mist that had entered from the main door. Behind the blue mist, the orange glow of the flickering lamps filled the hall with serenity.

Pinkoo flew away to get Shom, leaving Steve there all alone. There was not a soul in the hall, and that made him feel a little lonely, and scared. Before he could dwell on that feeling, a figure appeared from behind the mist. It was Shom, whose kind smile elated his spirit. "Come, my child."

Shom guided Steve right up to the marble lotus. "We are here to seek the blessings of Lord Buddha," said Shom, and he picked up a medallion kept at the feet of the gold statue.

The medallion looked like a piece out of an antique shop. It was made of a strange alloy. There was a thousand-petal lotus embossed at the center of this pendant. Around the lotus were seven gems, each a different color—the seven colors of the rainbow. The chain of the medallion was made by combining seven cords, each of a different metal.

Shom put the chain around Steve's neck. "It looks beautiful on you. For ages, this medallion has been passed from one generation of monks to the next. But only once in centuries comes a soul who is worthy of wearing it. I was told this story by my master, when I was your age. This medallion will give you the power to communicate with me anywhere, any time. Keep it on you always; never lose it."

As the medallion was placed around his neck, Steve felt a sense of well-being pass through his body. He involuntarily bowed before Buddha's statue, even before Shom could say, "Thank God for your good fortune, my child. Thank him, for you have been granted the wonderful honor of wearing this medallion. And remember to thank God for all that he has given to you. Thank him for all the happiness as well as all the pain that comes to you."

"I don't understand this Master. Why should I thank God for the pain I have got? If God loves me why does he give me pain?" Steve was not ready to accept Shom's words without clearing his doubts.

Shom smiled back as he knew why Steve asked this question. Any young boy his age, who had gone through such hardship, would not accept what he said. Wanting to help Steve come out of his painful past Shom guided him. "Let us say, while running a race you trip over a lose lace of your shoe and fall down. You don't just hurt yourself, you also lose the race? Will you thank God for it?"

"Of course not," said Steve instantly. "Why should I thank God for giving me pain and failure?"

"OK. Don't thank God for anything," said Shom, trying to pacify Steve. "But did this incident teach you anything?"

"Nothing," was the quick reply.

"Not even the fact that next time when you prepare for a race, tie your lace properly, so that you don't trip and hurt yourself again?" said Shom with a smile.

Steve was not prepared for this. He kept quiet for a while, thinking of an argument to support his point. "I will tie my lace, but still, why should I thank God for hurting me"

Shom was amused at Steve's innocence, "Wasn't it God who was watching over you while you were running? Had you not tripped, you would have not noticed your small mistake, and might have repeated it again my child," said Shom. "We don't see God, so we don't understand his presence in our lives. Every day, every moment, his loving eyes are watching over us. Sometimes, in certain situations, we are not able to understand why God gave us this challenge. But behind every incident, there is a bigger plan of our loving God."

This was a new thought for Steve, whose life had been full of challenges since his childhood. His curious mind still had unanswered questions. "But Master, why did I have to leave my friends and come here for no fault of mine?" he asked.

"I understand that leaving your good friends behind, for no fault of yours makes you feel sad," explained Shom. "But if you think for a while that you could make new friends here, you could get the company of everyone who loves you here; you freed yourself from the sufferings at the orphanage, you will see why God wanted you to come here. My boy, nothing happens to us without a reason. It's up to us to look at it the way we want. When we are grateful to God, for whatever he has sent to us, we invite more reasons to be grateful for. On the other hand, if we complain for the challenges that life brings to us, we bring into our lives more situations to complain for. This is a choice that we have to make. To be happy or to be sad is in our hands." Grand master Shom's words were truly comforting.

Steve smiled at Shom who gave him a warm hug and said, "Come, let's go now." Steve felt light and calm as they walked out of the Gompa. There was a dense mist outside and it was still dark.

"Hold my hand," said Shom. Steve blindly followed Shom as they walked through the mist. It felt just like the Trust Walk. Steve couldn't see anything. But though the ground was obscured, Shom did not fumble his way across it. He knew every turn, climb, and fall of the path to the Butterfly Nest. The unforgettable experience of the Trust Walk with Cheeka helped Steve now. He surrendered himself totally to his grand master and allowed him to take over the journey. This felt so comforting. Trusting, without doubt made things so easy for him.

Inside the dome, there was light all around. The little florescent green butterfly eggs glowed like a multitude of twinkling stars. Shom walked with Steve to the center of the dome, and they sat on the floral bench. They were silent for a while. There was no sound inside the dome. Not even the sound of the fluttering of the wings of the butterflies, which were still asleep. After a while, Steve heard the distant sound of a bird. As time passed, a few more birds starting chirping. Soon the walls of the dome started stirring. The butterflies were waking up. Finally, Shom spoke.

"Hear the birds and butterflies, Steve? It's time for them to wake up to another morning. A morning that will be very different for you and me. With the first ray of the sun, a new chapter will open in our lives. This will lead to the fulfillment of our purpose on this earth…yours as well as mine." Shom knew that Steve's young mind might not be able to completely comprehend what he was saying, so he added, "Don't worry, my boy. This experience will be the most beautiful and memorable experience of your life. Just be with me and do as I say."

Shom then looked up at the butterfly dome. All the butterflies were awake by then. They fluttered their wings and filled the Butterfly Nest with a soft breeze. Shom raised his hands toward them. "Oh blessed friends! The time has come for us to visit 'the Secret' once again. Please make way."

Shom held Steve's hand and guided him, "Stay on this bench, and do not move until I tell you."

The breeze created by the fluttering of the butterflies started getting stronger. Steve looked up and saw that the millions of butterflies that formed the dome had started to fly around in circles. Soon the entire dome was revolving and the butterfly breeze was turning into a strong wind, and before Steve could get a grip on what was happening, it turned into what could only be described as a tornado. Steve felt that he would be blown away. He held Shom's hand tightly and was visibly frightened. Shom clutched Steve's hand and said, "Don't panic, my child. God is taking care of us."

The tornado grew stronger, and all the plants and the glittering butterfly eggs started rotating in its tow. Soon even the floor of the Butterfly Nest was revolving. The twinkling eggs were swept up, creating a multicolored mist all around.

Steve and Shom sat on the floral bench, right in the center of the tornado. And though everything around them was revolving fervently, their seat was steady.

As the tornado reached an incredible, dizzying speed, Steve noticed a passage opening below their seat. From under the passage emanated a bright light. Gradually, the passage grew bigger and the light became brighter. The bright beam from inside the passage reached the top of the dome and spread all over. The radiance of the light was almost blinding. The tornado was so strong that under the pressure of its wind Steve could feel his skin flapping against his muscle and bone.

He looked at Shom, who seemed to be unaffected by all that was happening around him. His eyes were closed, as in a meditation. Steve closed his eyes out of fear. But then he realized that his seat, which had been steady until now, started to move. Startled, he opened his eyes and was shocked to see that the passage in the ground had grown into a huge pit, and his seat was floating over it.

The bright light took over the whole place. Everything, including the air and the essence of the Butterfly Nest, was now sucked into the large pit. Startled and scared, Steve looked at Shom again. His eyes were still closed, but while one hand gripped Steve firmly, the other signaled for him to remain calm.

Gradually, their floating floral bench was lowered into the pit. Steve saw the edges of the ground rise above them. The pit was shrinking. The tornado slowed down with the flight of the butterflies slowing down. Steve could never in his wildest dream imagine that delicate butterflies could create such energy. Gradually the butterflies came back to their natural pace of flying. Eventually they stopped, and the pit closed above them. There was darkness all around. It was completely silent. Everything was still.

As they sat feeling the silence after the roaring noise, for a brief moment, Steve thought he heard a faint buzz nearby, as if a fly was hovering around him. But before Steve could notice this unusual sound or draw Shom's attention, within seconds, the sound disappeared. However, it made Shom uneasy too. "Are you OK, Steve", he asked.

"Yes Master," said Steve, somewhat shaken, "But isn't it rather dark here?

Shom could sense Steve's concern. He quickly made an announcement, "Friends, can we quickly light up this place?"

Steve wondered who was Shom talking to. As if on cue, a spot of tiny light appeared in the darkness. It seemed to come from far below. The light reached closer, followed by many tiny lights like it. And then hundreds of tiny spots of light came floating in. They formed two rows, revealing a long staircase going down. Steve could not see where the staircase led to. As the lights reached closer, Steve discovered that they were glow worms. Their flickering lights lent a warm glow to the mystical staircase. Steve marveled at the unusual sight. He looked at Shom, who smiled back and said, "Come, Steve, let us start our journey into the heart of the Secret."

Steve looked down at the seemingly endless column of stone steps. He wondered how long he would have to walk to reach the end of the staircase. "Don't worry," said Shom "everything in this beautiful place is made for your comfort. Come, let's go down." Shom held Steve's hand and stepped on the first step. To Steve's great surprise, the stone staircase moved down like an escalator.

"There, my child! Didn't I tell you that everything here was made for your comfort?" said Shom. "These steps were built many centuries back. That civilization was far more advanced than today's scientific world."

The steps took them down a long vertical tunnel. Steve observed that the walls of the tunnels were engraved with various figures and forms.

"These murals depict the history of our civilization," explained Shom. Steve noticed that the figure of a warrior seemed to move, and it felt like the warrior looked at him.

"Don't worry," said Shom, holding Steve's hand. "These are guards who have safeguarded the Secret for centuries."

Shom continued to explain the meaning of the images they passed, until they reached the bottom of the staircase. In front of them was a wall of water, flowing from the floor to the ceiling of a hallway or tunnel.

Where does the waterfall come from? And how is it flowing against gravity? And where do we go now? These and several other questions were on Steve's mind. As if to answer them, Shom raised his hand and pointed his finger to the center of the water wall. The wall parted into two, from the center, like curtains. Shom and Steve passed through the space that was formed in between. Once they were on the other side, the water curtains pulled back to form the wall of flowing water.

Shom and Steve were now facing an inconceivable mirror maze. The entire space ahead of them was surrounded by unfathomable layers of mirrors, some fixed to the walls of the room, some suspended, mirrors of all shapes and sizes. Even the floor had steps and platforms made of mirrors.

And in this mirror room, floating in midair, were seven crystal globes that revolved in fixed, interconnected orbits. Every few seconds, the globes would glow from inside. Steve was fascinated by the crystal globes and reached out to touch one of them. It stopped in its orbit and, as a result, the other six bumped into it. Within a moment all the crystal balls skidded out of their orbit, dashing into one another. Steve was petrified. The crystal looked delicate and would surely shatter. He looked at Shom pleadingly. Shom rushed to stand between all the globes. He crossed his hands into an X. Soon the crystals returned to their original orbits, and then they revolved around Shom.

He stepped back and looked at Steve who was nervous with guilt and fear. "Don't worry, my boy. These globes may look delicate, but they are so strong that nothing can destroy them. They are here for an important cause. I will explain that later."

Steve let out a heavy sigh and looked around. All the mirrors were moving in different directions. The walls and partitions were moving, the layers of ceiling were moving, and all the steps and platforms on the floor were moving. Steve was amazed to see thousands of his reflections appear and disappear all around him. Then he realized that he could not see Shom's image in any mirror. He nervously looked around and saw that his Master was still standing beside him.

"Wondering which way to go?" asked Shom. Actually, Steve was wondering why he could not see Shom's reflection on any of the thousand mirrors! "Do you see that big mirror in the center of this room?" continued Shom.

'There were thousands of mirrors in the room. Which mirror is he referring to?' thought Steve.

"Look carefully, Steve," said Shom. "There is only one mirror in the center of this room that is not moving. See that one over there?" Steve finally located the only mirror that was not moving. Surprisingly, that was the only mirror in which he could see Shom's reflection. But he couldn't see his own.

"Don't be bothered by all that is happening, my boy. It

doesn't need to make sense yet," said Shom. "That mirror is our doorway to the Secret. Come with me."

CHAPTER — 7

AN UNBELIEVABLE ENCOUNTER

Shom walked up to the mirror as Steve watched him, wondering if yet another door would open inside it. But something inexplicable happened. Shom walked right into the mirror and merged with his reflection. Steve stood there, first marveling at what had happened, then wondering what he was to do next. From inside the mirror Shom extended his hand toward Steve. "Come, my child," said Shom, "hold my hand and enter the Secret!" A little scared, Steve walked toward the mirror.

Suddenly, he heard that buzzing sound again. Was it the fly that he had felt earlier, when they'd come down through the tornado's center? Was it just his imagination? Steve stopped to shoo it, when Shom asked again, "Is something the matter, Steve? What is bothering you?"

Steve forgot about the nagging fly and walked toward the mirror. Most of Shom's body was in the mirror, but his arm extended outside it. For a moment, Steve stood still, amazed by what he saw. When he went close to the mirror, he felt that it was not like any other mirror. At a closer look, under the surface of the mirror appeared waves that travelled at a high frequency. He looked at Shom's hand, but was not able to gather the courage to hold it.

"Come on, Steve." There was a sense of urgency in Shom's voice. "We have to enter the Secret before the first ray of the sun reaches it." Steve held his master's hand and simply walked into the mirror, as if there was nothing between him and the space on the other side. For a while he closed his eyes and stood silently to settle down. When he opened his eyes and looked around, a different world was awaiting him.

Steve felt like he had entered heaven. Before his eye was the most impressive marvel of architecture he had ever imagined. Everything was made of sandalwood, and its soft fragrance pervaded the majestic hall. On the front wall was an imposing sandalwood statue of Lord Buddha, sitting in a meditative posture. The statue was seated on a large lotus that had thousands of beautiful petals. It appeared so fresh that it looked as if it had just bloomed. In front of the lotus there were seven large golden eggs.

Numerous flowers, motifs and scriptures were etched into the walls of the hall. On both sides of the hall, huge intricately carved pillars—which appeared to be made of white marble—went up to the ceiling. But strangely, the pillars did not support the ceiling. They were about a couple of feet from the ceiling.

'What's the point of having pillars if they don't touch the ceiling?' thought Steve. 'Maybe they are merely decorative.' He was lost in the beauty and fragrance of the place when he felt the much awaited gentle pat on his shoulder. He looked up and as expected, he found Shom smiling at him.

"Welcome to 'the Secret', my child," said Shom. Mesmerized by the impact of the place, the imposing statue, the unusual pillars, the glittering golden eggs, Steve was in loss for words. Shom drew his attention again, "Do you like the place?" he asked. Steve was soon aware of his presence in that hypnotic space.

"It's beautiful. And so peaceful!" he said, his looks still fixes on the golden eggs. "But why is it called 'the Secret.' What's so secretive about this beautiful place?"

"That's exactly what I am going to tell you now," said Shom. "This is the place of God that protects the biggest Secret on earth. And the Secret is hidden in those gold-en eggs there." All this while, Steve had been wondering about the presence of the golden eggs in such an unusual surrounding. Now that he knew about them, he was even more curious.

"Centuries back, our ancestors made seven paintings, based on old scriptures that deciphered the power of the Sun God. These paintings were placed inside those seven golden eggs. Collectively, the seven paintings can be used to harness the power of the sun. This is a power beyond the imagination of the human mind. For a moment think of the power of the sun that can destroy anything remotely close to it. Anyone who acquires this power can conquer the world. If wrongly used, it can destroy everything on earth. All life, all vegetation, the mountains, the seas, the forests—everything will perish, in a matter of seconds. On the other hand, this great powerhouse of infinite energy can also be used for the betterment of humanity. If this pow-er is positively channeled, it will change the future of our mother earth. It can avert earthquakes, tornados, tsunamis, flood, famine and all other natural calamities born of global warming. Mass destruction and violence will stop forever, as no global power will dare face this super power. This energy can conserve nature and return earth to its bountiful past."

Steve listened in disbelief and amazement. Shom went on. "But in every age, it has happened thus: for every positive effort, there have been negative forces working against it. Down the centuries, evil powers of the black world have kept track of the Secret. They've made every effort to acquire it. And for generations we have tried to save it…which is why these paintings have been guarded so zealously."

This was not quite convincing to Steve. "If you've possessed this secret for centuries," he said, "why have you never used it, Master?"

"That is where you come in, my boy," said Shom.

"Me?" wondered Steve. "How come? I know nothing about these paintings."

"Let me explain," said Shom. "You know that the white light of the sun, as our eyes see it, is actually made up of seven colors—the colors of the rainbow."

"Yes," said Steve, though not too confidently. He vaguely remembered Aunt Susan, at the orphanage, telling him about the seven colors that were the spectrum of sunlight.

"Violet, Indigo, Blue, Green, Yellow, Orange, and Red," reminded Shom. "These seven colors come together to create white. And these seven colors are represented by the seven paintings. When these paintings come together, they create the supreme power—the white light of the sun."

Steve was intrigued, but he could still not understand

his role in this scheme of things. "So what do I do?" he asked.

"You are the only human being who is born with the power to convert the ray of the sun into the seven colors of the rainbow. That is why you have the seven rainbow lines on your palm." Shom explained. "The seven lines on your palm have an immense power that you are only now becoming aware of. These mystic lines will help to ignite the latent energy in these paintings. One by one, these seven paintings will bring to life seven creatures, each bearing one rainbow color. And then the Seven Creatures of the Rainbow will merge together to create the supreme power—the Sun God!"

"But there is a missing link in all this," Shom went on. "When our ancestors first succeeded in creating these paintings, they were fortunate to find a boy like you, who had the power to energize the paintings. But before the Creatures of the Rainbow could come to life, the boy was kidnapped by evil forces.

"Our ancestors fought hard and rescued six of the seven paintings, but could not rescue the boy. Without him, we could do nothing. And we still have no clue where the seventh painting is. So, for generations we have safeguarded the six remaining ones. They are in six of the seven golden eggs you see here." This was a lot of information for Steve. He was confused, scared and in disbelief of his powers that Shom was talking about.

Shom could understand the dilemma of the young boy. He soon comforted Steve. Putting his arm around Steve, he said, "Isn't it amazing to know about how special you are?"

Steve was taken aback by all this. He was not prepared

to accept it. "I like this place and the mystery that surrounds it. But Master, I am scared to hear all that you say about me. I am happy being the regular boy I am. In all these years I have got used to being pushed around and punished. Now that you talk such things about me, I can't believe it. I don't want to believe it. And why should I be special? I am OK the way I am."

Shom could see why Steve had that mind set. Having lived under oppression and poverty from early childhood, Steve's young mind was conditioned to a certain pattern of thinking. He had to help Steve, and so he went on in a more casual and convincing way. "Remember yesterday's Trust Walk, Steve?" he asked. "Yes Master," said Steve thinking of the amazing experience.

"Try to recollect what happened when you saw the rainbow near the waterfall," said Shom. Steve was quite shaken by the incident and preferred forgetting it. He kept quiet.

Shom went on, "At that point you could not understand it, because it was so powerful. But Steve, among all the other boys this happened to you because only you have the amazing Rainbow power." Steve kept quiet in disbelief. Trying to convince him, Shom added, "Remember how Mr. Arnold was thrown across the room in the bakery when he hit you on your right palm?" Steve hung his head in disgrace and fright, as he did not want to remember the dark past. "It was an accident, not my fault," said Steve in defense.

Shom went on, "That was not an accident Steve. And it was definitely not your fault. It was your Rainbow Power, the power you are born with. The power I have been talking about all this while. And for all these generations, we have waited for you to arrive, my child. Now you are here. It's time for a great change on earth."

Shom held Steve's hand as they walked toward the imposing statue of Buddha. He bowed before the statue. Then, looking upward, he closed his eyes and waved his hands in the air. Sparks, like fireworks, came out of his fingers. The sparks flew across the hall and struck the top of the large pillars in the hall. That's when Steve realized that the pillars were actually huge candles. The sparks from Shom's hands lit the candles, and in the glow of that warm light a third eye appeared on the forehead of Buddha's statue. The eye opened and emitted a beam of light that fell on Steve and Shom like a spotlight.

"Hold my hand, Steve, and look at Buddha's third eye," said Shom. "Right now, all the members of the Gompa can see us."

Outside the monastery, all the members had gathered in the courtyard. The sun was about to rise. In the orange-golden sky, the monks saw Shom and Steve, as if figures on a movie screen. Everyone bowed down to Shom, as they heard his voice float from his image in the sky.

"My fellow monks! Today is the day that we have awaited for centuries. In a few moments from now, we will present the Secret to you. And this is possible because we have in our midst the most precious link. Without him, we would have never seen this day. And this invaluable link, this bringer of good fortune, is young Steve!"

Everyone hailed Steve.

Shom continued, "As I said, Steve is most precious to us.

Therefore, we must vow to protect him, even at the cost of our lives. We are about to begin a new chapter in our lives. We cannot be sure about the turn of events. But whatever the outcome, always remember to protect Steve! May God be with us!" As Shom spoke these last words, their images disappeared from the sky.

Down in the sandalwood chamber, Shom gave some final instructions to Steve. "Now listen carefully, my boy. With your power, we are going to summon the creatures from the six paintings that we do have. When they are formed, they will attract their seventh companion from wherever it is." Shom held Steve close to him. "God is with us. He will take care of everything."

Shom led Steve to the center of the room, where the floor was painted with the image of shining sun.

"Do you see that small vent in the wall, above the head of Lord Buddha?" asked Shom. Steve nodded. "In a short while, the first ray of the sun will enter this room, through that vent.

"Raise your right hand, son."

Steve obeyed, not with enthusiasm, but with fear.

"When the sun's ray enters, it will hit your raised palm. You need to stand still, right here. Don't get disturbed; just observe what's happening.

"Bless you, my child. May the Lord be with you!"

Shom's words were assuring. But Steve could feel his heartbeat increasing steadily. He stood still, with his hand raised, waiting for the first ray of the sun to touch his palm. There was stillness all around. The wax from the huge candles had slowly started melting. The patterns created by the molten wax added to the mystical ambience.

Steve looked at Shom, whose eyes were closed. He was calmly chanting a mantra. The stillness of the room, the absolute calm pervading in the atmosphere, the mystery of the Secret unfolding and realizing of the power that he possessed within him, a power that can create peace or havoc, a power that was about to unleash through him, all this was too much of a pressure for Steve to handle. Years of struggle, hunger, insults and punishment had such a deep impact on him that this new world of love, of compassion, of empowerment scared him. Comfortable in his world of low esteem, Steve was not prepared to face the new world opening up before him. This was too much, too soon for him to handle. He gave up and lowered his hand.

Deeply immersed in his chanting, Shom felt a jolt. He opened his eyes and looked at Steve, who stood quietly, looking crestfallen and defeated. "What happened to you, my child," said Shom, visibly disturbed.

"I can't do it," was the short answer.

Shom remained silent for a while trying to understand what Steve was going through. He knew that they did not have much time in hand. The first rays of the sun would soon enter the room and if Steve did not cooperate, this chance would be lost. "How can I help you feel better, my child?" asked Shom.

"I am no good, Master," mumbled Steve nervously. "Please don't tell me about my powers. I am the same guy who can't bake a bun properly. I am the same guy who was punished for hurting Mr. Arnold. I am the same guy who was thrown out of the orphanage, to this far away land.

And here I am, getting all the attention I don't deserve, being told stories of all the power I am supposed to have. I know this can't be. I am not the guy you are making me out to be. Why are you doing this to me Master? I feel scared standing here raising my hand, waiting for a miracle to happen. I know nothing will happen. Please…punish me, for not obeying you, beat me if you want. That is what I am used to. But please don't take me through this useless drill," saying this Steve had tears in his eyes. He had kept silent for too long. But so much of love and goodness was more difficult for him to digest, than being ridiculed and hated.

Shom kept silent. He could understand that years of pain had made Steve believe that pain was his reality. Anything outside this world of sadness was false. At this point, inflicting anything on Steve, no matter how true, or good it was for him would make things worse. "OK. It's perfectly fine not to do what you don't feel like doing," Shom's words put Steve at ease. "Come, let's take a walk and explore this place. There is so much to discover."

Steve quietly followed Shom as they went near the candles. At a closer look, the candles appeared to be intricately carved. The design was so fine that Steve wondered what sharpness of vision and precession of craftsmanship it would require to achieve such perfection on wax. "Aren't these beautiful?" asked Shom, noticing Steve's interest in the carvings on the candles.

"Indeed, Master, this looks likes the work of a master…a great…," said Steve trying to find the right word to admire the outstanding carvings.

"You are right, they are master craftsmen," said Shom,

"And do you know who these master craftsmen are?" Steve was curious to know. With a gentle smile Shom said, "They are young boys, some your age and some slightly older than you. Most of them are from similar or worse backgrounds than yours. But that's not all. The unique thing about them is that they have no eye sight. They are blind."

Steve was shocked. "What...I mean how...How can this be possible?" he said in disbelief.

"This can be possible if you 'believe' that you can do it. These boys 'believed' they could carve a beautiful design without eyesight, just by touch, and by following what their heart really wanted," said Shom. Steve was too over-whelmed to talk.

"We are all born with a unique gift from God," Shom continued with love and compassion in every word. "No one is given everything under the sun by God. If we lack something, God compensates it with something much bigger. Like these boys, who lacked eyesight, but had the unique talent to create masterpieces on these candles, knowing that it would melt and they will create yet another masterpiece. So, my child, just like the art of craftsmanship that these boys are born with, you are also born with your own unique talent, the Rainbow power. It does not matter how big or small your power or talent is. What matters is realizing the unique role you are supposed to play in mak-ing our world a better place. And of what use is that talent or power, if you yourself do not recognize it and 'believe' in it?" Shom's words came as a bright light at the end of a dark tunnel where Steve was groping to find a way.

"I understand what you had gone through in the orphan-age for all these difficult years. But wasn't that yesterday?

Today is a new day. A day to smile and know that you are unique, that you have a power that is meant not just for you but for so many others. And most importantly, 'believe' in your power. It's a gift of God."

In a moment everything seemed to change for Steve. What seemed impossible a moment back seemed to be the only truth. Everything appeared so easy and Steve gave the sunniest smile to Shom. "I Believe"! said a confident Steve.

"I knew it, my boy," said Shom with a broad smile as he looked up and added, "Thank you God."

Quickly both went to their first position. Steve took a deep breath of confidence and raised his hand in anticipation of the first ray of the sun. "That's my boy," said Shom and started chanting. Steve could feel the serenity of the surrounding. He felt connected to the Almighty and eagerly awaited the miracle to happen.

Then, with a click, the lid of the vent opened. It brought in a whiff of mist into the room. And finally, piercing through the mist came the first golden ray of the morning sun. It travelled straight to Steve's palm and seemed to dissolve into him.

Steve had never experienced this sensation before. He could feel the rays of the sun traveling through every vein in his body. He could feel every cell of his body absorb the rays and come alive. Steve could see his body glow with a golden light. Filled with renewed energy, he declared to the universe, "I BELIEVE IN MYSELF!" Then he felt something moving on his raised palm. It was the rainbow lines pulsating with life. Each line dazzled with a different color of the rainbow.

First, a violet ray emitted from Steve's palm and spread around a beautiful violet hue. Then a soft indigo ray traveled beside the violet ray. This was followed by a blue ray and then the green, yellow, and orange rays. Finally the red ray completed the rainbow. It was the most magical rainbow Steve had seen. Each ray was alive with sparkling stars of the same color, traveling across the path of the rainbow. Steve was mesmerized.

"Steve." Shom's calm call broke the trance.

With complete attention, Steve followed Shom's instructions. "Keep your palm upright. But slowly lower your hand. Move it down until your hand is at the same level as Lord Buddha's feet."

Steve saw that as he lowered his hand, the rainbow moved from the head of Buddha down his body to his feet. In this process, the statue itself transformed. Just above Buddha's head, a violet halo appeared. The halo then morphed into a beautiful lotus with a thousand petals. Then Buddha's forehead glowed with an indigo hue. In this way, all the colors of the rainbow traveled down his body. The wonderful sandalwood statue of Buddha appeared to have come to life.

"Well done, Steve," encouraged Shom. "Now point your rainbow toward the seven golden eggs at Buddha's feet."

Steve lowered his hand further. The rainbow traveled with his hand, and as it reached the golden eggs it branched into its seven colors—each color touching one of the seven eggs. Each egg, in turn, absorbed and glowed with the color shining on it. Then each egg slowly split into two halves.

Very old-looking paper scrolls glided out of six of the split eggs and floated midair.

All the while, Shom was chanting. When the paintings were out and floating, he said, "Now focus your rainbow on the floating scrolls."

Steve followed the instructions, as if in a hypnotic spell. As soon as the colored rays touched the scrolls, they unfurled, revealing six intricate paintings.

Instead of paper, the scrolls were made of the thin bark of some kind of tree. The color of the bark had dulled. But the ink and the colors still looked fresh, especially the gold, silver, and copper paints, this gave the paintings a magical shimmer. There were no discernible figures, only scripture and geometrical shapes, arranged in some kind of pattern. When the rays of the rainbow touched them, the scriptures and shapes started moving. They moved faster and faster within the borders of each painting, until they seemed to merge into one another and take a form.

Steve could now feel the strain of keeping his hand in the same position for all this time. He was beginning to lose his concentration. But then he was struck by what was happening in the paintings. By now each one was completely soaked in its respective color, and Steve thought he could see little puffs of colored smoke oozing out of small pin holes in the paintings. Yes! The patterns and scriptures on each painting had merged into one another and were now morphing into tiny clouds of colored smoke. What an amazing sight it was! A cute baby cloud would pop out of corner of a painting and float in midair, changing shape, while another one would jump up from another corner and join the first one. This play of the cute colored 'cloudies' went on until they came together into a human-like form.

The smoke from the violet painting took the form of a wondrous creature. Its body was like two roly-poly lumps of cloud, one on top of the other. The smaller smoky lump on top was like the face of a newborn baby, with large innocent eyes. The cloudy body glowed from within and almost appeared stuck, half in and half out of the painting. Steve watched in awe while this creature looked down on itself and pushed a pair of hands and feet out of its smoky body. It smiled shyly and pulled its hands and feet back into its torso.

Steve's eyes moved to the five other paintings and found that similar creatures had emerged from them. Each one was a small, hazy, humanoid being bearing a different color of the rainbow. They were unlike anything Steve had ever seen. All six creatures jumped from their paintings into the golden eggs below them.

Lost in awe of the Creatures of the Rainbow, Steve had forgotten about his raised hand, until he heard Shom's voice. "You can lower your arm, Steve. See and enjoy God's wonderful creations."

"I love them, Master," Steve said. Then he added excitedly, "Can I touch them?"

"Not yet, my child," said Shom. "Right now we are just one step away from the great realization. But we will have to wait for our six little friends to attract their seventh brother. Then our journey will be complete."

"Your journey shall not stop, my friends! I have come to give you the missing link!" A deep, hoarse voice boomed from behind them, shattering the tranquility of the sacred place.

CHAPTER – 8

THE INTRUDER

In a moment, everything changed. Steve saw fear in the large, innocent-looking eyes of those little creatures as they jumped back into their paintings. They soon took the form of tiny colored smoke puffs and merged with the colors of the age-old paintings and disappeared.

Shom and Steve turned, in shock, to see a striking, tall, lean figure behind them. There was something undeniably fearsome and evil about this man. His long face had a pointed nose and thin lips painted white. Under his shaven eyebrows were big, drugged-looking eyes with thick, bushy lashes. The steep forehead was painted red. And on the head was thick, long hair, knotted at its end. Above his head hovered a bunch of bats, flying in circles to create a black halo. A long, thick beard extended all the way to his knees. He wore a long and flowing black gown, and over that a garland of human baby skulls. There were dazzling rubies pierced into his earlobes. In his right hand, he held an ivory staff that had the figure of two mating snakes of gold, and a big diamond on top.

Steve was immediately reminded of the menacing bats

he had seen on the Trust Walk and outside his window in the moonlit night. He trembled in place, petrified. Shom sensed Steve's fear and drew him closer. He himself sounded uneasy and confused as he confronted the man.

"Who are you? And how dare you set your foot into this protected abode of God?" Shom demanded.

"Shom, my friend!" said the intruder in a voice that seemed to come from a deep tunnel.

Steve could see that Shom was shocked that the man knew his name.

The intruder continued, "To answer your first question, my name is Koraka and I worship the Satan through the sacrifice of living beings. I come from a corner of this planet where mankind has never been able to set foot – the Bermuda Triangle. Proudly, I carry the legacy of my forefathers, who believed that this world is meant only for the powerful to exist. For this noble cause if the week needs to be sacrificed, they might as well be sacrificed. You can see testimony of these sacrifices on this garland that adorns my neck." Koraka's proud, resounding voice sent a chill down Steve's spine. "And your second question—how did I enter this fiercely guarded place? The answer is simple. Like this!" Koraka snapped his fingers and disappeared.

Steve and Shom waited in suspense, wondering where Koraka could have gone. Then Steve heard the same buzzing sound that was bothering him when he entered the chamber. The next moment, he saw a small fly with a red head, flying right in front of his nose. Though small, the fly looked fierce as it flipped rapid flames through its wings. Steve felt the intense heat from the flashes of fire digging into his skin; his eyes were not able to withstand the harsh waves from the fly's hypnotic eyes. He clenched his Master's hand tightly and tried to hide behind his robes.

"Buzzz...Remember me?" said the fly as it came uncomfortably close to Steve. Drops of sweat appeared on Steve's forehead as he was unable to hide his nervousness.

"Leave the boy alone", demanded Shom, "or else....."

"Or else what?" snapped the fly. "Relax, old man... Don't be so protective about this weakling. Let him burn his fingers a little, while he grows." Saying this, the fly swiftly circled around Steve's head, creating a ring of fire.

"I said Stop it," shouted Shom. For the first time since he had met Shom, Steve felt anger in his voice.

"As you wish," smiled the fly as it transformed and took Koraka's form again.

"Impressed?" asked Koraka proud of the display of his powers. "Now, tell me Shom, does this answer your second question?" asked Koraka with a crooked smile.

Shom had not finished. "I am not done yet," he said assertively, "Why are you—"

"No...no...no...my friend! Koraka does not answer more than one question at a time. You are special to me, so I obliged you by answering two. Now it's my turn to ask you something very important." Koraka paused to watch their reaction. "What will make you really, really happy right now?"

"To see you out of this sacred place, right away," said Shom, getting impatient.

"Wrong answer!" said Koraka with a scornful smile. "What will make you really, really happy...is THIS!"

He drew out a scroll from the sleeve of his long gown,

a scroll that looked much like the six paintings Steve had seen earlier.

"Now tell me honestly. Doesn't this painting make you really happy?" Koraka grinned, showing off all his repulsive yellowed teeth. "This, my friend, is your missing link – The seventh painting, the seventh Creature of the Rainbow—the Red creature. For ages, your monastery has protected the six paintings of the Rainbow, while my poor ancestors could lay their hands on only one. But this is one hell of a valuable painting, and it happens to belong to me. Without this painting, your seventh Rainbow creature will never exist. Unfortunately, the rest of your six creatures are useless without just this one gem of a possession. Now isn't that something to be proud of?" Saying this, Koraka kissed the painting.

"Come to the point now," said Shom. "What exactly do you want?"

"Now you are talking," said Koraka proudly. "I want a share of exactly what you want. A share of the supreme power that you were planning to enjoy all by yourself! Haven't you heard, 'Sharing is caring'…Um?" Koraka smiled wickedly. "Imagine the things we can do together with a power like that. All nations, whether rich or mighty, will bow before us. Together we can rule from any corner of the world. You won't even need your poor monks of this forsaken monastery to boss over, Shom." Koraka went on wickedly. "Or would you rather keep playing ping-pong with your six smoky creatures and their cute golden eggs? The choice is yours, my friend!"

Shom kept quiet for a while. It was clear to Steve that Shom did not want to be party to anything with this evil man. But Koraka was not really looking for agreement. His plan was well worked out.

"Don't worry, Shom. If you do not agree to join hands with me, I have another option for you." Saying this, he clapped his hands thrice and looked up at his bats. "Come… come, my darling blood suckers. Look what Papa has got for you." The whole bunch of bats started hovering in circles around Koraka, but no one dared to come near him. Suddenly, in a flash he caught one, and squeezing it in his strong grip, he said, "Now why on earth do you have to remain away from Papa when he has ordered you to come to him?" The bat was choking under his tight grip. "Urrgh… Master, pl…pl… please spare me. Mis…Ugh…Mistake, my Master! Big Mistake!" Koraka gave him a sinister smile, "Have you forgotten…My Wish….." The bat quickly completed the sentence, "Your wish…Urgh…is my command, Master!"

"That's better," said a satisfied Koraka. "Now here's what I want you to do," he continued, "See the majestic candle burning royally in that corner?" The bat strained to look in that direction, "Y…Yes…Ugh… Master," was the short, frightened reply. "Good," said Koraka, pleased with the bat. Handing over the painting to the bat he added, "All you have to do is to take this right up to the flame of the candle and wait for my orders." The bat obediently flew with it to the top of the burning candles. "Now, Shom," he added, "Say no to my offer, and the last painting will be turned to ash."

"Stop!" shouted Shom. "Bring back the painting and place it where it belongs—at Lord Buddha's holy feet."

"So be it!" announced Koraka. "My little black

beauties bring me the painting." The bats obeyed their master. Koraka gave the painting to Shom. He took it solemnly, walked silently to the altar, and placed the painting at the feet of Buddha. He then turned toward Koraka.

"We are ready for the great moment!" he said to Koraka. "As you understand, the whole process is very precarious. We can't take any risk and can't have any movement in this room. So may I request that your bats stop hovering over your head?"

Koraka readily agreed. He snapped his fingers and the bats settled down, some on his shoulders, some on his hands.

When the fluttering of the bats was over, Shom closed his eyes to meditate. But suddenly he heard a shriek.

"Aaargh!" It was Koraka. "You thirsty blood sucker! Can't you have patience? I'll fill your tummies when all this is done."

Rubbing a fresh bite mark on his hand, Koraka turned to Shom. "This is why I keep the bats in the air all the time. Sorry for the interruption, my friend. Please continue."

"His dreams are filled with greed and hatred," Steve heard Shom saying. But, like during the initiation rituals, his lips were not moving. Koraka could not hear Shom, or so it seemed, because he just stood there grinning away at them.

Shom took Steve's hand and they turned toward the statue. Then, again without speaking, Shom told Steve, "If this wicked Koraka possessed the super power of these united paintings, he would destroy the world. Pray with me, Steve, that we may protect the power from going into the wrong hands. May we hide this power from evil eyes."

Shom stood motionless for a while, with his eyes closed and hands folded in front of him, deep in prayer. Finally, he opened his eyes and smiled at the statue of Buddha. He looked pleased. With gratitude, he bowed before the statue and faced the sunrays coming in from the vent. His body was absorbing the rays and glowing like the sun. Shom raised his hands, which now seemed to emit the light that his body was soaking up. From the tip of his fingers burst out hundreds of delicate rays, like the early reaches of the morning sun. Gradually he clenched his fist. As the pressure on his fist grew, the rays became bigger and stronger, shining brighter and hotter, like the midday sun.

Suddenly, Shom turned his fist and the blinding rays towards the giant candle at the base of which Koraka was standing. In a matter of seconds, the entire candle was melting. Before Koraka could react, wax was falling all over him and his legs were completely buried and stuck.

"What have you done, you traitor? I trusted you!" he shouted as he struggled to lift his legs. The wax poured on him relentlessly. His bats tried flying off, but their wings were stuck. Their shrieking cries pierced every corner of the room.

"You have made a grave mistake, Shom!" Koraka shouted, now waist-deep in wax. "You have no idea what I can do! You underestimate my powers, Shom!"

"Your powers can never be greater than the powers of the Lord," said Shom calmly, as the strong rays from his fist kept melting the wax pillar at an alarmingly fast pace. "These painting are sacred, and Lord Buddha will never allow them to be with a greedy man like you. You want to use the power for your own greed, to enslave humanity. So remain buried here, at the feet of God, until your heart is clear and your intentions are right. I will pray for you."

Shom went on melting the wax with his powerful rays, without a pause. By now, Koraka's body was completely submerged under the molten wax. Only his head could be seen. But he didn't stop trying to wriggle out, and he didn't stop his threats. "I warn you, Shom! Nothing on earth can confine Koraka for long! You will repent this! Koraka is born to rule the world! The universe shall bow down at my feet one day! And you shall perish under my powers! I promise you that!"

Koraka's death-like yell resounded in the hall. He opened his mouth and took a big, long breath, gathering all his energy. His eyes became red and fierce. Then he opened his mouth and blew out a storm of flames. Like thunderbolts, the fire from his mouth hit all the other candles. The flames of the candles surged, swelling into monstrous bonfires. The candles started melting down, and soon the entire floor was covered with wax. Koraka's mouth, ears, and eyes were covered in it, and with the last of his breaths he spit fire and shouted, "Now you are doomed, Shom! And so is that nitwit kid! This is the molten grave for those paintings, too. Die a painful death. We will definitely meet in our rebirth. Farewell!" With these last words Koraka and his bats were completely buried under the wax.

CHAPTER – 9.

NO WAY OUT

hom had to act fast. The other candles were melting rapidly. Shom rushed to the altar and picked up the seven paintings. He took one last look at Buddha and bowed at his feet. He then turned to Steve. But Steve was not in his place. For a second, Shom froze with fear. "Steve, my child, where are you?" There was no response. The boy was most precious for him. "Where are you, Steve? Answer me, my boy!"

The melting wax and flaming candles made huge crackling sounds. But there was a faint sound amidst all that noise: "Speak up, Steve. I can feel your presence in this room. Speak up, child!"

Shom was getting desperate. Suddenly a giant candle fell and created a huge wave in the sea of wax. Shom was so lost in his search of Steve that he did not notice the wave of molten wax rushing towards him. Before he could react, his feet were quickly submerged under the hot wax. He knew he could not float on air any more. However, he did not bother about himself and called out for Steve as loud as he could. "Do not panic, my child. Your master will save you. Just call out, Steve!"

"Master!" Steve's faint voice was heard amidst the chaotic noise.

"Steve! My child," said a panicked Shom.

The scorching wax was up to Shom's knees, but he did not seem to care about his pain. "I can hear you, my boy! Where are you?" Shom called out.

"I'm here, Master!" Shom heard Steve's voice from behind a giant candle. He mustered all his strength and moved in the direction of the voice, fighting against the wax that burned every inch of skin that it touched, the paintings clutched tightly in his hands. As he approached the candle, he spotted Steve and was relieved to see that he was standing on a table.

"Ah! My child! Thank God you are safe." Shom hurriedly picked up Steve in his lap. "We must get out of this place right now!"

Shom rushed through the burning lava-like wax, which was now up to his waist. Steve could see great pain in Shom's eyes, but Shom wouldn't relent. He kept wading, making sure that Steve and the paintings were above the wax.

"Help me, my Lord," prayed Shom. "Help me reach the mirror maze."

With all the vigor he could summon, Shom rushed toward the entrance of the mirror maze. In the meanwhile, suddenly two more towering candles fell into the molten wax, creating a series of massive waves in that horrifying sea. The waves came together, rose up to the ceiling, and traveled toward Shom. With all his might, Shom leaped toward the entrance of the mirror maze, pleading in prayer, "Mercy, my Lord. Mercy!" He stretched to touch the huge mirror at the entrance of the maze, and instantly they were sucked through. The huge wave of wax lashed against the mirror, which remained unaffected by its impact. The boiling lava of wax fast filled the entire hall on the other side.

But inside the mirror maze, everything was tranquil and silent, as if nothing had happened. Shom looked around to ensure that everything was safe. Nothing had been touched in the mirror maze. The mirrors were intact and moving in their positions. The seven crystal globes rotated on their axes. Having ensured that they were safe, Shom lowered Steve on to the floor.

"Thank the Lord that you were not harmed," Shom said to Steve. "We have very little time left. First, we have to secure these paintings and take you to a safe place. Let's hasten to the crystal globes."

Shom then realized that his feet were stuck. The molten wax was solidifying on his body and gluing him to the ground. Soon all the wax would dry and set him to the floor. Shom took in a deep breath and closed his eyes. With a ripping sound, he freed his legs in one strong motion—leaving the skin of his feet behind. The peeled skin stuck to the wax on the floor as Shom staggered forward.

Steve looked away from the gory sight. Shom did not even wince. "Hold my hand, Steve, and take me to the crystal globes."

Steve took him to the center of the mirror maze, where the seven crystal globes were rotating. Shom could not stand on his feet any longer. He went down on his knees and handed over the paintings. "Now listen to me carefully, my boy. One by one, place the paintings on each of the seven globes. Place them in order, from Violet to Red." Steve followed Shom's instructions. As soon as the seven paintings were on their respective crystal globes, the paintings were sucked inside them. Each globe glowed with the color of the painting. Shom looked at the globes with contentment.

"These paintings will not be secure in this place," he said in a weak voice. "In these globes they will scatter to seven corners of the world. Only you will be able to locate them."

Shom closed his eyes, folded his hands in prayer, and started chanting. As the chanting continued, the globes rotated faster. The intensity of the chanting increased, and so did the rotation of the crystal globes, until they reached a climax and the globes became a blur of spinning light. Before Steve knew it, they vanished. Shom collapsed to the ground, while Steve looked around helplessly.

On the other side of the mirror maze, the hall from which they came looked like the site of a volcanic eruption. Half the room was filled with molten wax, boiling like lava. The heat was tremendous, and it was destroying everything around. The walls and the sandalwood carvings were charred. The beautiful sandalwood furniture had turned into ash. Most of the giant candles had melted, and the rest would soon melt and fill the room completely with wax. The only thing that remained unaffected was the sandalwood statue of Buddha.

Suddenly, there appeared a stirring in the wax, somewhere in the center of the room. It looked like a whirlpool, gradually growing in size. Soon, from the center of the whirlpool appeared a dazzling diamond. It glistened like the sun as it rose. Then, attached to the shining diamond, came out the face of two golden snakes. The golden snakes glistened in the brilliance of the bright light all around and revealed the magical staff of Koraka. And as the whirlpool grew deeper, out came Koraka's hand, holding the staff. And the next moment, everything changed.

A blast of ice and snow burst out of the diamond and launched into the room. The freezing snow collided with the fire and molten wax. There was thick smoke all over. Nothing was visible except the glistening diamond and the glowing golden staff. Thunder, lightning, and heavy snow spread across the room, clashing with the heat and fire. In a few moments, the wax was frozen solid. For a while, everything was still. And, then the room started shaking, as if struck by an earthquake.

The tremors reached the mirror maze as well. Shom, nearly unconscious, opened his weak eyes. He staggered to his wounded feet. The solid layers of wax clung to his burnt body. He saw that the crystal globes were gone and Steve was in a state of shock. The tremor in the mirror maze grew in intensity.

"Come to me, Steve," said Shom in a feeble voice.

Steve was too shocked to move.

"Come to me quickly, my child. We have no time to lose." Shom's energy was dwindling fast.

The tremors grew. The moving mirrors stopped in their paths. The glass floor started shaking. Steve could not gather the courage to move.

"Don't just stand there, Steve." Shom's voice was weak but firm. "Come to me, immediately."

"Yes, Master," Steve obeyed. But as soon as he tried to move, he fell onto the shaking floor.

"Be brave, Steve," said Shom. "Get back on your feet and come to me."

Steve was willing to do anything that his master asked him to, no matter how afraid he was. He walked, fell, crawled, as the floor shook violently. Somehow, he finally managed to reach Shom.

Shom held Steve's shoulder and leaned on him. "Pay attention to every word that I am saying. The crystal globes have carried the paintings far away, to seven different parts of the world. They are hidden where no one can find them. No one, but you!"

Suddenly the floor shook so hard that Shom lost balance and came down on his knees.

"Help me, O Lord!" Shom pleaded in pain. Steve did his best to help his master back up. "You need to act quickly. There is a map that shows the way to the seven destinations of the paintings. The map lies in the Valley of Flowers. To locate the map, you first need the secret scroll that is kept under the seat of Lord Buddha's statue, in the hall, where you enter our Gompa. Take that scroll to the Valley of Flowers, and—"

Before Shom could complete his sentence, there was a big blast in the hall that completely shook the mirror maze.

The rock-solid wax in the adjacent hall started cracking from the impact of the blast inside it. The cracks grew bigger and wider as the whole place shook violently, and the huge mass of wax seemed to fall apart. Soon there was another blast, sending solid lumps of wax flying across the room. And from inside the wax burst out the vampire bats. Finally, Koraka emerged. It seemed as if the fire and molten wax had no impact on his body. His vampire bats were also unaffected. Boiling with rage, Koraka dashed toward the mirror maze.

Inside the mirror maze, Shom apprehended the approaching danger. "Steve, it's time for you to leave this place."

"No, Master! I will not go without you," pleaded Steve.

"I am grounded. Your life is precious, my boy. And remember the sacred medallion you wear. It will always be your tool to connect with me from any corner of earth. Never lose it. Now leave this place before something happens to you."

"I can't leave you like this," said Steve adamantly.

"I command you to go, right now!" Shom raised his voice.

Just then, there was a blast at the door of the mirror maze. A huge ball of ice crashed into the mirror maze, breaking open the door. In came Koraka, screaming at the top of his voice. "No one goes out of this place! Now listen, you betrayer, I have not come here for child's play. Before things get worse, hand over the paintings and the boy to me."

"The paintings and the boy are sacred. And sacred things do not go to the evil," said Shom sternly. "Your evil intentions have brought you to this holy place. But you can never go out of here. As for Steve, he is God's child, and will find a safe passage out of here." Shom turned and said, "Steve, leave this moment."

Steve started moving toward the water screen that was at the entrance of the mirror maze. But a furious Koraka ordered, "Steve! If you move another inch, I will destroy you."

Steve stopped in panic, but Shom insisted, "Go, Steve. Run! This evil man cannot stop you. The Lord is with you."

Steve ran toward the water screen. Koraka lifted his staff in rage, and a sharp beam of ice blasted out of it and toward Steve. With his last bit of strength, Shom jumped into the path of the ice beam.

Steve heard the blast and turned to see what caused it. He saw Shom standing between Koraka and himself. Shom had stretched his arm toward Koraka and a powerful blast of light had countered Koraka's beam, pushing him back. In the process Shom's feet were frozen to the ground. But Koraka had also lost control over his powers. Shom turned toward Steve and pointed his finger at the water screen, which split. Steve ran up the stairs, and the water screen closed behind him. Koraka tried to aim another blast of ice at Steve, but it struck the water screen and turned it to a wall of ice.

As he continued up the staircase, Steve could hear blasts against the ice wall. Steve turned to find that the wall was growing thicker and thicker and would not relent. Faintly, he heard the voice of Koraka: "Nothing has ever stopped Koraka! Nothing can ever stop me from getting what I want! Least of all, you, Shom. I had promised you death. And death you shall get."

Steve was gripped by immense sadness as he heard Shom's feeble voice—a voice that he could hear more in his heart than in his ears—"Life and death is only in the hand of the Almighty. No human being has this power. And one who tries to take this power in his hands is doomed. As for you, Koraka, you have sinned, and God will punish you," said Shom calmly.

"Enough of your sermons!" shouted Koraka. "Your end is near, Shom. Prepare to die!"

Steve ascended the staircase and emerged from the secret passage. Exhausted and confounded by everything, he staggered through the Butterfly Nest, came up to the courtyard of the monastery, and fainted. There was total darkness before his eyes.

In the mirror maze below, Koraka pointed his staff at Shom. One blast of ice and Shom would perish. But before Koraka could act, Shom waved his hands in the air. Millions of stars sparked from his fingers and hit all the mirrors in the maze. The sharp edges of the stars shattered the mirrors, and the shards plummeted and sped toward Koraka. His bats scattered while the pieces of mirror collided with their master and formed a multi-layered glass cage tightly around him. The impact of the mirrors was so hard that Koraka dropped his staff. The bats fled through the vent behind Lord Buddha's statue. The pieces of the mirror clung to Koraka's body, squeezing him from all directions in a body-tight cage. He could not move an inch.

Everything was absolutely still.

CHAPTER – 10.

THE SEARCH BEGINS

Inside a deep, dark tunnel emerges a small beam of light. It is flickering at a distance. Gradually the light grows stronger as it comes closer. The beam enlarges and spreads through the darkness, and the black fades into white. The white light becomes brighter and brighter until the darkness totally dissolves in it. Now there is white light everywhere. Gradually, the light turns into snow. And the snow grows in volume. Heaps and heaps of snow that starts turning into ice crystals and crystals turning into ice cubes. The ice cubes multiply from hundreds to thousands to millions, until they become huge blocks of ice, which then grow into a wall of ice. And the wall grows bigger and stronger. It seems impenetrable. But, suddenly a sharp ray pierces it from the other end. The ray is blinding bright. It keeps drilling deep into the wall of ice. Slowly, cracks develop in the wall. The cracks widen as the beam continues to pierce the ice wall. Finally, a huge blast shatters the wall into tiny crystals of ice again. With the explosion, a blast of molten wax springs from behind the shattered wall of ice. The lava like wax gathers momentum as it travels toward

Steve. He is taken by surprise and looks around in panic, his eyes searching for his Master. But Shom is nowhere to be seen. Steve wants to call aloud, but is shocked to realize that he has lost his voice. In the mean time, the lava like wax has come very close to him. Steve has no choice but to run from the approaching danger. But to his utter shock he finds his feet stuck to the ground. He looks down and freezes with fear to see two powerful hands of Koraka holding his feet in a rock solid grip. Steve is bathed in perspiration. He struggles hard, but the menacing grip of the evil man gets harder. Finally, Koraka lifts Steve up and throws him into the boiling lava of wax......

"Master....Help!" shouted Steve as he woke up with a jolt. His eyes tried to adjust to the rays of the morning sun falling on his face. He looked around. Everything seemed misty and hazy. He could make out that he was in a room where everything was white. He was lying on a white block of marble, covered with a white bed sheet. The only source of light was a small vent from where the golden rays were diffusing into the mist in the room. The sunrays and the fragrant mist were soothing to Steve's frightened and tired mind. It felt like he was waking up from a horrible nightmare. He looked to his left and saw a big marble statue of Buddha lying beside him. The imposing statue scared him, and he was about to scurry to his feet when he heard a voice. "Take it easy, Steve. You are safe here, in God's house."

Steve recognized the face, as the monk came closer. He was Vyoma, the senior monk who had taken the boys for 'Trust walk' trek.

Vyoma smiled at Steve and affectionately caressed his hair. "How are you feeling now?"

"Don't know," was Steve's answer. "I'm feeling kind of lost and exhausted."

"I can understand, Steve," said Vyoma. "You had a tough time. But God is kind; you are safe."

"How is Master? Is he…?" Steve could not complete the question, as tears rolled down his cheek.

"Our master is safe," assured Vyoma.

"How do you know?" asked Steve.

"He communicates with us from where he is now. Right now, he is where you had seen him last—inside the mirror maze. He is stuck with the evil Koraka. He will have to remain there. Otherwise, Koraka will escape. But don't worry, Steve. Our master will always be safe, because the Lord is taking care of him."

"But how do we get him out of there?" Steve was not satisfied with Vyoma's reassurance. "Master must be hungry, thirsty, and in pain!" Steve winced as he remembered Shom's burnt leg, with its skin peeled off.

"No, Steve." said Vyoma. "Our master is beyond hunger, thirst, and pain. The incident was unforeseen. It was too sudden and since you were to be saved, our master was hit accidentally. But he can't remain in this state forever. He has the power to heal himself. He is in the service of God, and God will take care of him."

"No…Sorry, but I don't believe in God anymore," said Steve in despair. "Ever since I have come here, I have been hearing Master say that God will take care of everything. If there is God, why do things go wrong? Why did Koraka enter the 'Secret' and destroy everything? Why did our Master have to suffer such pain? Where is God now? Why doesn't he come to our help?"

Vyoma could understand and feel the pain Steve had gone through. He wanted to help Steve come out of the state of shock he was in. "You are right, Steve. I agree with you," Vyom lovingly caressed Steve's hair as he continued.

"We don't see God. And we are so used to believing in things which we can physically see, that it's difficult for us to accept something that is not there before our eyes. But think about it Steve, when we complain about why certain things happen in a certain way, when we question the presence of God in a situation beyond our control, are we not wanting to see his presence? We actually want to believe that there is a force, call him God, or Lord, or Buddha, or Christ...a power that will come to our rescue when we are stuck in a helpless situation. But when this does not happen, we challenge his presence." Steve kept listening to Vyoma, though not willing to understand his point.

"For a moment, imagine a situation where Master could not save you and in the struggle both of you got buried under the wax. Isn't this better than that? What if Koraka had got hold of all the paintings and fled, leaving us helpless? How would that be? In such a situation what have you heard our elders say?" asked Vyoma.

"God Forbid," was Steve's quick reply.

"Isn't that accepting the presence of God?" asked Vyoma with a smile, as he continued, "Sometimes, we are not able to understand the ways of the Almighty. What appears unacceptable to us now might be holding within it a lot of good that we are not able to see. We condemn it because it has not happened the way we would have liked it to be. Isn't it?" asked Vyoma smilingly. Steve listened to him with attention. This was something he had never thought. In fact, no one had ever talked to him like this.

Vyoma came closer to him and asked, "How did you feel when you had to leave the orphanage?"

"Very sad, very angry," said Steve.

"But had you not come here, would you have made such good friends? And imagine discovering your Rainbow power here, in our monastery? How wonderful is that?" asked Vyoma. "I guess I had not thought about it all this while, but it actually feels much better here," said Steve, with a smile as things appeared quite different now.

"That is how God wanted it to be for you," explained Vyoma, "Things appear to be much easier when we leave it to God to take care. We call it Faith…a belief that whatever is happening, is happening for the highest good. There is a power that is taking care of us, of everyone and everything. Once we start thinking like this, we receive the good out of every situation. And that state of surrender, my boy, is what we call 'God'."

Steve kept silent for a while. He was trying to understand all that Vyoma had said. This was so new to him that the child in him would take time to assimilate it. His heart was still craving to somehow save his Master. He could not stop himself from asking, "But can we all not go together inside the Mirror Maze? We could capture Koraka and save our Master." Steve was desperate.

Vyoma was amused by the boy's innocent insistence. "It's not that easy, Steve. You have just come out of the place and you know the state it is in. Our master has blocked it in a way that no one can step in. However, right now, our first concern is to find the seven paintings. Master told me that only you can go on this mission; no one else can touch those paintings. We will support you in every possible way. But it's your journey, my child."

Steve fell silent for a while, wondering how he could fulfill this big an expectation.

"Don't worry, my boy," said Vyoma, as if reading his thoughts. "The longest journey starts with a single step. Have faith in God. Don't brood over it right now, because you are in great company. See who is here?"

Cheeka, who was waiting outside the room, came in flaunting his wrinkly-eyed smile. Steve and Cheeka hugged like they'd been separated for years.

"I'm so glad to see you, Cheeka," said Steve.

"Me too!" said Cheeka, smiling at him.

"Someone else is glad too, Steve!" said a tiny, familiar voice.

Steve smiled. "Pinkoo! Where are you?"

"As always…I am here!" Pinkoo said playfully.

Steve knew where to look for Pinkoo. He turned to his right shoulder, and there she was. Pinkoo fluttered her wings and sat on Steve's nose. "How is my best friend feeling now?" she asked.

"Now that you're here, I'm absolutely fine. But when I went to the…" Steve stopped midway, not sure of how much he could tell his friends.

Vyoma sensed Steve's dilemma. "It's okay, Steve. You can share all you want with them. Master wishes that you have them as your confidantes. But don't stress yourself right away."

Vyoma was about to leave the room when Steve interjected, "Master told me about a secret scroll which is kept under the seat of Buddha, in the hall. I need to find that scroll."

"Yes, Steve," said Vyoma, "but you need another day's rest. Relax and enjoy it with your friends. We will start afresh tomorrow."

Steve spent the day with Cheeka, Pinkoo, and other friends in the monastery. They went to the hot waterfall and bathed for a long time. The hot water and the fresh air washed away all his pain.

Steve shared his adventure with Cheeka and Pinkoo. "Master risked his life to save me and the paintings," said Steve. "Now I have to find them in seven secret places of the world. Master said that there is a map in the Valley of Flowers. Have you ever been there?"

"Yes, of course," said Pinkoo excitedly. "All the butterflies from the Butterfly Nest go to the Valley of Flowers to collect their nectar. But I haven't seen any map there!"

"You're right. I don't remember seeing any map there either," said Cheeka, a bit confused.

"We'll go there tomorrow," said Steve. "But I need to carry the secret scroll to the Valley of Flowers. Will you two come with me?"

"Of course!" was the chorus. "First thing tomorrow morning!"

It was still dark and misty outside, as Vyoma guided Steve, Cheeka, and Pinkoo to the entrance hall. Behind the mountains, the sky was gradually getting brighter. Birds had started chirping. The group walked in silence. Steve noticed that Vyoma was carrying a big magnifying glass attached to a long silver stick. They entered the hall in silence. Like every time that he'd been there before, Steve was filled with a deep sense of peace and tranquility.

The incense sticks that were always burning in the hall were emanating smoky whiffs. Long, flowing, white curtains that covered the statue of Buddha appeared mysterious, as they swayed without any breeze. Vyoma took the children across the hall and up to the marble lotus. Vyoma touched his forehead to the white lotus, and its petals opened and revealed the holy water within it. They applied the water on their eyes.

The white curtains had moved aside to reveal the serene statue of Buddha. Vyoma set the long silver stick in front of the statue, such that the big magnifying glass faced Buddha.

"Now, let us sit in silence and meditate until the first rays of the sun enter this hall," instructed Vyoma.

Steve and Cheeka sat on either side of Vyoma and closed their eyes to meditate, while Pinkoo sat on Steve's shoulder and followed suit. For a while, there was absolute silence.

Then an unusual sound, like the tinkling of glass, echoed in the hall. Steve opened his eyes and looked in the direction of the sound. The tinkling sound was coming from the large magnifying glass. The morning ray of the sun had touched the magnifying glass and passed through it, forming a spectrum of colors. The multicolored rays of the spectrum converged again into a dot. This beautiful dot of light touched the Buddha's forehead, just between the eyes. Gradually, the dot grew bigger, and the golden statue started glowing.

Steve looked around to find that Vyoma was still deep

in meditation. Cheeka and Pinkoo, as wide-eyed as Steve, were staring at the statue.

And just then, the statue started to turn around and shift from its base. As the statue moved, it revealed a gold box underneath.

Now Vyoma opened his eyes and spoke. "Collect that box, Steve."

Steve picked up the box and carried it back to where he had been. Vyoma then walked up to the statue and removed the magnifying glass from its stand. As the converged spot of light moved away, the statue of Buddha turned back to its original position.

Vyoma opened the gold box and pulled out a scroll from within it. Though the scroll appeared ancient, it was intact. As Vyoma opened it, Steve noticed that it was made of a very unusual cloth. The cloth was transparent. At the center of the cloth was a map of the world. But it was no ordinary map. The borders of the countries and all other objects appeared animated. The clouds traveled, the winds blew, the oceans were vibrant with waves, the sun was rising, and the moon was setting. The topography of all the nations were shown to the last detail—from the mountain to the plateaus, the rivers and the lakes, the fields and the deserts, the snowcapped peaks of majestic mountains to the boiling lava in the erupting volcanoes. It was like our bountiful earth, in all its diversity, waiting to be discovered.

"What kind of a map is this?" Steve asked Vyoma.

Vyoma smiled at him and said, "This is the secret scroll. It's a unique guide for anyone who knows nothing about our world. A gateway to the discovery of our planet. It holds within itself the history, wisdom, and knowledge of all the ancient civilizations."

"But I can't understand anything. There's no cities or anything," said Steve. "It's just mountains, fields, rivers, deserts, oceans, and volcanos. How would I know where to start, and which way to go? And what about the paintings? This doesn't show where they are."

"Remember what Master told you. The secret of the seven destinations is hidden in the Valley of Flowers," said Vyoma. "This map is just a tool in your expedition. It shows the vast and glorious field in which you will now commence your quest. Most importantly, this map is alive and deeply linked to Mother Nature. It will warn you against approaching natural calamities and other dangers in your route. It will protect you against any evil forces that might harm you. This is God's gift to you. Take extreme care of it.

"Now it's time for you to go with this scroll to the Valley of Flowers. From here on, it's your journey. You have to proceed on your own. You always have our blessings. May God be with you!"

"I have a request to make," said Steve. "Could I please take Cheeka and Pinkoo with me? Without them, I will be lonely."

"I suppose you can. They have been your partners ever since you came here. You three can be one another's support on this expedition. I wish you all success." Saying this, Vyoma blessed them.

With clothes and food in cloth bundles, the three of them left for the Valley of Flowers. Both Cheeka and Pinkoo knew the route. They went behind the monastery and took the narrow lane that led to a forest. The forest was dense, with tall trees and thick bushes growing all over. A light wind blew through the trees, making a soft whistling sound. Sunlight filtered through the branches, creating hundreds of patterns along the path. Dry leaves crackled under their feet, breaking the otherwise silent ambience.

As they moved forward, the trees grew taller and denser. Their branches and leaves were so thick and interwoven that the rays of the sun could not penetrate them. The forest was dim, but they moved on.

After walking a little longer, they reached what seemed to be a dead end. The path ended abruptly at a steep rock face. There was no way they could climb this high precipice.

"What do we do now?" asked Steve. "Are you sure we are on the right path?"

"I can fly over this," said Pinkoo. "The Valley of the Flowers is on the other side of this rock face. I have been there many times with the other butterflies from the Butterfly Nest."

"But how do we go there?" Steve was worried.

"Nothing is impossible when you are with Cheeka!" said Cheeka grinning. "Come with me." Cheeka took them a few steps to their right, into the forest. Passing through the thick bushes they spotted the hollow trunk of a tree. It seemed that the tree had been felled. It had two hollow branches on either side. There were no leaves on these branches. The trunk of the felled tree must have remained there dry and hollow for several years. Steve wondered how this one tree could have been cut in a forest that seemed so untouched!

Cheeka stood at the end of one of the dry branches and said, "The Valley of Flowers is not a natural valley. It was created by one of our great masters, several ages ago. The flowers have been planted especially for all the butterflies of the Nest. This place is not known to other people. If they knew, they would take away all the flowers, and our butterflies would go hungry. So a secret passage was created from here to the other end of this huge rock. In this jungle we don't cut trees. Master always says that nature is like our mother. It feeds us, gives us rain, it protects us always. We should also respect and protect it in return. This hollow tree trunk that you see here has been artificially made. Inside it lays the entrance through the rock. Now, Steve, go stand near the other branch of this trunk."

Steve did as Cheeka said. Then Cheeka took out a small iron ball from his bag. The ball was old and rusted. It had six iron spokes of different sizes on its surface. Showing the iron ball to Steve, he said, "This iron ball is the key to a huge lock that lies within this trunk. When I roll it into this branch, the six spokes will open six levers inside the lock. Once all the levers are open, the iron ball will roll out of the branch beside you. Then the rock behind you will open. We will have to enter the tunnel that lies hidden behind this rock surface. The entrance remains completely open for just fifteen seconds. There are three of us, so we will have to rush. If one of us is left on this side, that person will have to stay back. The lock can open only once in twenty-four hours."

Steve and Pinkoo listened to their friend as Cheeka continued with the instructions. "Remember, as this key rolls down this branch, there will be six clicks—the sound of the six levers opening. After the sixth click, the iron ball will pop out at your end. Catch it and run toward the tunnel. Get ready, Steve. Here we go!"

Cheeka put the iron ball into the hollow branch. The sound of the rolling ball could be clearly heard. Then it stopped, and a "click" was heard.

"One," counted Cheeka.

The ball rolled on and a second click was heard, and then the third, fourth, and fifth clicks. Then for a few seconds the ball stopped rolling. Steve heard something rumbling behind him. He turned around to see a huge boulder shaking, as if it might fall off the rock face. The rumbling sound kept growing. Cheeka screamed to get Steve's attention back to the grave task at hand. "Don't turn, Steve. We can't afford to get distracted. Keep your eye on the branch. The key will pop out any moment!"

But, by the time Steve turned back, the sixth lever had already clicked and the iron ball popped out. Steve was taken by surprise and dropped the ball. Behind him, the huge rock started opening up.

Cheeka rushed to Steve. "Where did you drop the iron ball?" he asked in panic.

Steve was groping for the ball among the dry leaves under his feet. "It must be somewhere here."

"We can't afford to lose a second." The tunnel was now fully open. "In the next ten seconds the door will close!"

But Steve could not find the ball. "Forget it!" said Cheeka. "Let's rush into the tunnel."

The rock started to close and the boys ran towards it with all their strength. It was more than half closed when Cheeka jumped into the now narrow opening. He somehow managed to pull Steve into the tunnel, just before the rock completely shut with a big bang.

Cheeka and Steve turned to look ahead into the tunnel. It was pitch black.

On the other side of the rock, as if out of nowhere, a vampire bat appeared. It hovered for a while and then dived into the dry leaves, picked up the iron ball, and flew away.

CHAPTER – 11.

GROPING IN THE DARK.

Steve could see nothing. He could hear only his own breathing. He called out, "Are you there, Cheeka?"

"Yes, Steve, I am here. We were lucky to get in at the last moment."

"And Pinkoo?"

"I don't know."

Cheeka and Steve called out in unison. "Pinkoo!"

There was no response.

"Pinkoo! Answer me, Pinkoo." Steve was getting worried. "Stop playing pranks in the darkness. Speak up, Pinkoo!"

Only silence.

"Pinkoo is not here, Steve," said Cheeka. "I think she could not make it."

"How can that be possible? She is so tiny and fast. She has to be in here somewhere." After a pause, he added "Can't we go out and look for her?"

"There is no way that we can go back, Steve. We can only go forward. We have got to get out of this suffocating tunnel."

"No way. I am not moving an inch without Pinkoo!"

"So be it. You stay as long as you want. But I am leaving this place before breathing becomes impossible." Cheeka started crawling toward the other end of the tunnel.

Steve was terribly frustrated. He did not want to lose Pinkoo. But he also knew that searching for her in the darkness would be futile. Left with no choice, he followed Cheeka.

The tunnel was low and full of twists and turns, and the floor was rough. The boys were scraped and bruised on their way. After struggling for quite a while, they saw light. The end of the tunnel was in sight. That's when the journey became easier. Within a couple of minutes, they were on the other side of the tunnel. And when Steve stood up, the view before his eyes seemed worth all the trouble they'd had in the tunnel.

As far as his eyes could see, there were flowers. There were beds of white roses, spreading endlessly on all sides. In between the white flowers there were spurts of bright color—red, blue, orange, and yellow buds. The flowers seemed to be arranged in beautiful patterns.

The sweet fragrance of these flowers drifted throughout in the valley. Steve had never dreamt of so many beautiful flowers in one place. Enchanted, he closed his eyes to feel and breathe in the magical fragrance. Then a voice whispered into his ear, "Where are you lost, Steve?"

Steve opened his eyes and turned to see Pinkoo sitting on his right shoulder. "You!" he shouted, surprised, and then a little annoyed. "Where did you go? We were looking for you everywhere in the tunnel. Why didn't you reply? I knew you were playing a prank."

"But I was not in the tunnel," said Pinkoo. "I wanted to make sure the two of you had entered, and I ended up being left behind."

"So how did you get here?" Steve did not know whether to believe her.

"Didn't I tell you that we butterflies regularly fly over the hill to reach here?"

"Are you two done with your greetings?" interjected Cheeka. "May I suggest that we move on?"

"Okay. What's next?" asked Steve, as he looked around to figure out the way ahead.

"You need to find clues that will lead you to the seven locations where the paintings are hidden," reminded Pinkoo.

"Yes, and both of you need to tell me where to look for those clues. After all, you've been here before," said Steve.

"Yes, I've been here a couple of times. Every week, one of us is sent here to check on the flowers. But we've never been told about any hidden clues," said Cheeka.

"So what do we do? Where do we start?" Steve wondered aloud. He turned to Pinkoo for help. "What do you say, Pinkoo? You've come here a lot, haven't you?"

"Yes, but we've only come to collect nectar. I never guessed that there could be hidden clues here."

"These are age-old secrets that were not told to us," said Cheeka. "Only our grandmaster knew it."

"Well, then maybe we should just search everywhere," said Steve. "Without the clues our map is useless."

That reminded him of the map he was carrying with him. "The map! Maybe this will help."

He took the map out of his cloth bundle and spread it

before them. The transparent map was still alive, with flowing rivers, swaying trees, gushing waterfalls, and lashing waves. But there was no indication as to which of those routes would lead to the paintings. The only thing that was different was a golden star that shone at the north corner of the map.

"This is where we are," said Cheeka. "This is our guiding star that will always indicate our location."

"But the map doesn't explain anything," said Steve. "Like I said before, we'll just have to search everywhere in the valley. Should we search for the clues among the flowers?"

"No, Steve," said Pinkoo. "The flowers are reserved for the butterflies. No one but butterflies can touch them."

"So what do I do? Stand here and gaze at the beautiful flowers forever?" Steve was getting increasingly impatient. "I am going inside. Are you coming?"

Cheeka was still reluctant. "Our grandmaster always stopped us from entering the valley. He used to say that we selfish humans have kept everything exclusively for us. But none of us ever bothers to keep anything exclusively for the birds and animals, the butterflies and insects. Let us not enter the valley. It might harm the flowers."

"I am not going in to pluck flowers, Cheeka. I just want to find my route to the paintings. And there is nothing wrong with that, is there?" Saying this, Steve moved ahead.

"No, Steve. Don't go ahead!" warned Pinkoo.

But Steve continued walking toward the flowerbeds. And as soon as he set foot among the flowers, thorny creepers grew out of the rose plants and twirled themselves around his legs. If Steve moved even an inch, the thorns would prick him. As he stood there, rooted in silence and in pain, he felt that the only way out of this hopeless situation was to ask for guidance from his grandmaster. He was reminded of the medallion given by Shom. He held the medallion in his right palm and stood in a silent prayer. Soon the seven gems of the medallion started throbbing in a rhythmic vibration and Steve was startled by a voice.

"Steve, my child, impatience will never help you." Steve knew that it was Shom's voice. "The Valley of Flowers is sacred. It was made only for the butterflies of the Butterfly Nest. If we contaminate the flowers, where will the butterflies go to collect nectar? Don't worry. You have our dear Pinkoo with you. She will be able to help you…out of these thorns, and also to the clues."

Steve turned toward Cheeka and Pinkoo. That's when they realized that he was stuck and hurt. They rushed to the edge of the flowerbeds. Cheeka pulled on Steve's hand but couldn't get him out. Pinkoo sat on Steve's shoulder, and then, as if by magic, the thorny creepers left Steve and he easily walked out of the flowerbed.

"Thank you both," said Steve. "Sorry I lost my patience." Then he turned to Pinkoo. "Grandmaster spoke to me and said that you could help us find the clues."

"If that's what Grandmaster says, so I shall." And Pinkoo flew over the flowers. She went from one flowerbed to another in search of some clue, but could not find any. Steve looked at her flying about zealously and was suddenly filled with hopelessness—the valley was immense and Pinkoo was just a little butterfly. How could she possibly cover every inch of it?

But Pinkoo was undeterred; she checked every inch she

could. Within minutes, she was visibly exhausted and had slowed way down. Steve and Cheeka watched her from a distance but could not help her.

Steve was now more concerned about her than about the clues. "Why don't you rest for a while, Pinkoo?" he said.

"I can't afford to," she answered firmly. "You know that we have little time, and there is so much of the valley still left to search."

"How about you fly higher and get a bird's-eye view of the whole valley?" Suggested Steve. "Or should I say a butterfly's-eye view?"

Pinkoo laughed as she moved up a bit. It looked like it was not easy for her. But she gathered all the strength she could and moved even higher. Suddenly, she stopped mid-air. "Yes! I think I found it!" her feeble voice screamed in excitement.

But the boys could not hear her clearly. "Sorry? Can't hear you, Pinkoo. Why don't you—"

Before Steve could complete his sentence, Pinkoo continued prattling. "Steve, this is unbelievable!"

The boys were clueless what she was trying to say. They couldn't even figure out if she was happy, sad, scared, or just ranting from exhaustion.

It was Cheeka's turn to get impatient this time. "Hey, princess, flying up above the world so high. We mere mortals standing on Mother Earth have gone deaf. Could you kindly step down to talk to us?"

Pinkoo sensed the irritation in Cheeka's voice and flew back to the boys...unaware of the bat flying high above her. Pinkoo fluttered her wings in exhilaration as she chanted,

"It's amazing, it's just amazing! How could I never notice this wonderful secret hidden in the Valley of Flowers?"

"What is it?" asked Cheeka.

"The clues! They are all hidden in the flowerbeds," said Pinkoo.

"Well, what are they?" asked Steve.

"I can't explain it from here;" said Pinkoo, "you have to see the flowerbeds from up there to understand."

"In that case, all I need is a pair of wings!" said Cheeka sarcastically.

"Come on, Cheeka," pacified Steve. "Don't get so irritated. Without Pinkoo's help, we'd be nowhere." Pinkoo glided and perched herself proudly on Steve's shoulder. "We should actually try to understand what she wants to say. Let's see... we need to a get a bird's-eye view of the flowerbeds..."

Steve turned around, hoping to find some way. His eyes stopped at the rock face through which they had come. "Yes, we should climb to the top of the rock face," he said. He picked up the map and headed for the rock, with Pinkoo on his shoulder. Cheeka followed, still a little agitated.

They studied the rock for some time, only to realize how impossible it would be to climb it. There were no trees or craggy edges to hold on to. The boys stood there looking at each other. "Where do we start?" asked Steve.

Cheeka's weariness was apparent in his unenthusiastic response. "I don't know. I don't think this is good idea. I can see no path, nothing to hold on to. And we have none of those mountaineering gadgets."

"But if the flowers of the valley have been arranged to indicate a route, and the flower arrangement can be understood only from up above, then there has to be a way to reach the top of this great rock," said Pinkoo, whose spirits never seemed to dull. "The grandmasters of our monastery must have created something. We are surely missing it."

"I agree. Let's think about all that we've seen of this rock face," said Steve. "How about we go back to the tunnel's exit, where we came out?" His partners agreed.

On reaching the exit, they realized that the mouth of the tunnel was closed with a big boulder. There was no visible sign of any path leading to the top of the hill. The boys looked around for some outlet or clue. All they could see were stones of different shapes and sizes. They picked up stones and moved big rocks in search of clues, but could not find any. Pinkoo also tried to help, but because of her size she couldn't help much. But then she noticed a small rose plant with a blooming red rose. Strangely, the plant was growing on a rock.

Pinkoo's butterfly senses were very attracted to the rose, so she went and sat on it. She was startled when the plant started to creep back into the stone. Frightened, Pinkoo flew away and watched the plant from a distance. It disappeared into the stone, and then the stone started to roll. It rolled for a while until it hit a large rock next to it. And that rock slid away with a great rumble. The boys turned and saw Pinkoo pointing to the rock. There was an old brass handle hidden behind it that was now in plain view.

"What's going on?" asked Steve.

"I have no idea," said Pinkoo. Then she described what happened when she'd sat on the red rose.

Cheeka was familiar with such events. "If I'm not

mistaken, this should be the key to another passage," he said. "But it could also be a trap. Let me pull this knob and see what happens." He pulled the handle with all his strength, but nothing happened.

"Let me give you a hand," said Steve. The boys tried with all their might, but again nothing happened.

After thinking for a moment Cheeka turned it to the left. With a creaking sound, an inch of the handle came out of the rock.

"Let's turn it to the other side," said Steve. They did, and this time the earth beneath them started shaking. A fat column of rock, the brass handle at the top, slowly lowered to the ground like a drawbridge. It was a smooth cylinder of rock, and as it came out a huge crack formed in the rock face behind it, from the base to the very top.

Steve clutched Cheeka's hand, afraid that they were about to witness an earthquake. But Cheeka felt otherwise. "This is our path to the top." Cheeka's positive self was back in place.

"If this crack is a path, how do we walk through it?" wondered Steve.

"There has to be something more," guessed Cheeka. "Is it possible that…"

Before Cheeka could say it, the rock cylinder, which had fully extended and was now parallel to the ground, slowly rolled up the crack.

"This is it!" said Cheeka excitedly. "Steve, this cylinder will take us to the top of this rock. Let's hop on to it."

"How?" wondered Steve.

"We've got to give it a try. If we miss this chance, we might never be able to climb up. Just jump on. We can balance by walking against the direction that it rolls."

The rolling cylinder scraped and shook the rock face with billowing smoke and a deafening roar. The ground shook, too, and bits of rock and dust were falling all around. Steve was reminded of the horrifying experience he had had in the chamber of the Secret. He was too nervous to move.

The cylinder was picking up speed. Cheeka knew that there was no time to waste. He grabbed Steve's hand and jumped onto it. But Steve was unprepared and did not land on his feet. Cheeka couldn't get a grip on Steve's hand and had to concentrate on balancing on the cylinder. Steve rolled off, six feet above the ground. He would have come crashing to the ground, but he managed to grip the brass handle at the end of the cylinder. But the handle had become very hot because of the constant friction of the rocks. His hand started burning and he could not bear to hold on to the handle any longer. By now the cylinder had picked up speed and was rushing up the hill. Letting go now would mean falling down more than a hundred meters. Steve had no choice but to shift his grip from one hand to the other. But he didn't know how long his other hand could bear the pain of the burning handle either.

On the rotating cylinder, Cheeka was also struggling. As the cylinder ascended it rotated faster, which meant he had to walk backward at greater speed. The smoke produced by the friction of the stones had grown so heavy by now that he was losing sight of Steve. He could not see Pinkoo either, and wondered where she had disappeared.

"Steve, can you hear me?" Cheeka's voice seemed swallowed by the loud noise of the moving rock. While continuing his backward tightrope walk on the cylinder, Cheeka extended his hand downward and shouted even louder than before. "Give me your hand, Steve!"

"I can't see you, Cheeka!" said Steve's voice.

"Never mind, my friend. Just extend your hand." Somewhere in the smoke he could faintly see Steve's hand. Cheeka bent as much as he could.

As Steve reached, his other hand's grip on the handle kept loosening. Finally, Steve gave up. He could not bear the terrible heat of the brass handle. He let the handle go.

"No! Steve, no!" shouted Cheeka in desperation as he failed to get a grip on his friend's hand. Shaken and shocked, he saw Steve's figure disappear behind a thick cloud of smoke. In no time Steve would hit the rocky surface of the ground below. After a fall from this height there was no chance of survival. Suddenly, all the noise and movement stopped. The cylinder had reached the top of the mountain.

Cheeka stepped out and sat at the edge of the rock face, exhausted. The cylinder rolled back down the mountain and returned to its original, vertical position. The rumbling sound faded out. Cheeka sat silently on the rock, tears rolling down his eyes. His mission had come to an abrupt and terrible end. He had lost his friend Steve, and there was no sign of Pinkoo either. He stared blankly at the thick cloud of smoke that was still surrounding him.

As Cheeka sat in silence, he felt a gentle breeze blowing all around him. Gradually, the wind got stronger. The smoke started clearing. The wind's speed picked up rapidly, and

Cheeka was not sure what was happening. Strangely, the wind was not blowing sideways; it seemed to come from the earth below the mountain. Soon the wind grew into a storm, and the smoke totally disappeared. And this time, Cheeka stared with complete amazement!

From under the mountain appeared millions of butterflies, holding each other's hands. The "storm" was the wind caused by the fluttering of their wings. But the real surprise was yet to come. As the great net of butterflies came up, Cheeka was dumbfounded to see Steve in the center of it. His dear friend was alive and safe. And so was Pinkoo, who was sitting proudly on Steve's nose. The wonderful butterflies brought him to the top of the mountain and placed him softly on the ground. Cheeka was overwhelmed. He rushed toward his friend and hugged him.

"Steve! Steve, you're alive! I thought I had lost you. I'd have never forgiven myself for not being able to save you." Cheeka's voice was trembling with happiness. "How did this miracle happen?"

"It's all thanks to Pinkoo! As usual, she was there at the right time!" Pinkoo proudly fluttered her wings on Steve's right shoulder.

Steve began narrating the tale of being saved by his dear friends, the butterflies of the Nest. "The handle became so hot I had to let go. I closed my eyes and was prepared to crash to the ground, but instead it was like I bounced on feathers. It was very breezy, almost windy. I thought I was already dead and flying toward heaven when I heard Pinkoo's voice. I opened my eyes to see her lovely face smiling at me. I realized that I'd landed on these million butterflies!

"Pinkoo had rushed to the Nest to get them when she saw that I hadn't landed on the cylinder. I'm alive thanks to her." Overwhelmed with emotion, Pinkoo hugged Steve's nose with her wings. Steve kissed her bright pink wings affectionately.

An overjoyed Cheeka hugged his friends. The butterflies spread out around them, filling the space with myriad colors. The queen of the butterflies flew up to Pinkoo and placed a crown of golden petals on her little head. All the butterflies flapped their wings, creating a fragrant breeze all over.

"We are very proud of you," said the queen. "This is with a wish for all success always."

She then flew up to speak to the boys. "We are aware that the three of you are on an important mission. God's blessings and our master's grace will support you. We shall always be there with you. Now it's time for us to collect nectar. We must bid farewell for now."

The queen was just about to fly away when Pinkoo called out, "Please, Queen, don't go now."

"Why?" asked the queen.

"If all of you go to collect nectar, you will block Steve's view of the valley. We've come up here to get a bird's-eye view of the flowers, which have been arranged in a certain pattern."

"So be it, my child," said the queen.

She motioned for the butterflies to make way, and the boys walked past them to the edge of the rock face.

"Look carefully," Pinkoo told her companions. "The entire valley is filled with white roses. In between these white flowers are bunches of colored flowers. And these bunches of colored flowers are joined with green shrubs. Doesn't this look like some kind of design?"

"Yes, you are right," said Cheeka as his eyes brightened. "The flowers are set in the order of the colors of the rainbow. It starts with the color violet and ends with the color red. Did you notice that, Steve?"

"Of course," he said. "These are the seven colors of our seven paintings. And the green shrubs joining these colors indicate some kind of a route." said Steve as he quickly took out the map and spread it on the ground. Everyone studied the map carefully. As usual, everything in the map was animated and a golden star showed their present location on the rock face, facing the Valley of Flowers. But they could find no similarity between the patterns of the flowers in the valley and anything on the map. Pinkoo flew into the valley and back to the map several times, looking for answers. Finally she gave up and sat on Steve's shoulder, completely downcast.

The queen butterfly was watching all of this, a bit confused. "Why are you looking at the map and flowerbeds separately?"

"What do you suggest we do?" asked Steve.

"The map is transparent, isn't it? Why don't you look at the flower patterns through the map?"

This was a great suggestion. Steve took the map to the edge of the mountain. Steve and Cheeka lifted it in front of them, and through it they could see the whole valley clearly. The map swayed and wiggled in their hands. Steve and Cheeka held on to it tightly, fearing it would fly out of their hands.

The queen butterfly saw this and said, "The map is not

flying away because of the breeze. The wind around us is soft and gentle. The map looks like it needs to free itself. Let it go!"

Steve and Cheek let go of the map. It rotated, midair, and halted such that the flower patterns fit exactly with markings on the map. Through the transparent map the boys could see seven destinations clearly marked in seven parts of the globe, and routes—the green shrubs among the flowers—that connected the seven destinations. Gradually, the impression of the flower patterns got imprinted on the map and the map flew back into Steve's hand.

The butterflies fluttered their wings again and the boys were overjoyed. The queen flew into the sky along with all the other butterflies. They filled the sky with colors and formed different patterns, and finally they wrote "Good Luck" in the sky. Steve, Cheeka, and Pinkoo waved at them as they stooped down to the flowers to collect nectar.

The sky was clear and the sun was shining bright. The boys took a closer look at the map. Their first destination was marked by the first color of the rainbow, Violet. This destination was in Alaska. Steve had heard of Alaska and its difficult terrain. Now the question was, How do they get there? They had no means of transport.

"Well, at least we have the map and know about the seven destinations," said Steve.

"But we don't know where to start."

Both the boys went silent. Pinkoo watched the sadness that was creeping into their faces.

"Why are you so sad?" she asked.

"Look how difficult things appear," said Cheeka.

"Will this sadness help you?" asked Pinkoo calmly.

The boys had no answer to that.

"You know this mission has been given to us by our master. There has to be a way to solve every problem on this mission," asserted Pinkoo.

"That's right," said Steve. "If only Master was around to tell us what to. Everything appears so difficult without him."

"But hasn't Master guided you whenever you needed help?" asked Pinkoo. Steve nodded. "So why don't you trust, and ask him for help?" suggested Pinkoo.

Steve nodded again, sat down calmly, held his medallion and closed his eyes. Cheeka and Pinkoo followed him. In his mind and heart, Steve concentrated on Shom. And as he sat in deep meditation, Steve did not realize that a dozen pairs of eyes were watching him and his friends; up in the sky were lurking Koraka's bats, spying on everything that the trio did.

Unaware of this, Steve held the medallion communed with Shom. "We are at the first step of our mission and are stuck. How do we proceed with the long journey ahead of us?" All three friends desperately wanted an answer.

The touch of the medallion and the thought of his master calmed Steve down. And from the depth of his heart he heard Shom's voice. "My child, you took the first step toward this mission when you left the Gompa, with everyone's blessings. And all three of you have already made good progress. As far as the rest of the journey is concerned, the map will guide you. And do you forget that God has given you the power of the rainbow? Remember how you took the rays of the sun on you palm to bring the paintings to life? Remember your powers. The rays of the supreme power—the sun—will help you. The rest of the journey will automatically unfold before you.

"And most importantly, have faith in yourself, my boy. Believe that you have achieved your goal, start living the moment and feeling the success as if you have already achieved it and success will be yours. May God be with you always!"

There was a long silence. He opened his eyes and found the map floating in the air in front of him. The sun was shining brightly. Cheeka sat calmly, and Pinkoo, as usual, was on his right shoulder.

"Cheeka, Pinkoo, let's prepare to go. Hold my hand." Steve raised his right palm toward the sun. As the sun-rays touched his palm, they energized the rainbow on his palm. It started glowing, and the violet ray from the rain-bow came out of his palm and touched the violet spot on the map. The violet ray bounced back from the map and covered the trio. The ray grew more intense. A huge storm broke out, starting from the violet spot on the map, and all three of them started floating over the map. They held each other tightly. The storm grew and pulled them toward the map. And before they could realize what was happening, they were sucked into it.

All the trio could see was violet. They were drenched in it. Then they started traveling. In a hollow violet space, they were moving at an unimaginable speed. Steve had read about the speed of light. He felt that he was experiencing it right now. It felt like traveling through space. He could only describe as 'absolutely unreal.'

Then, the violet color started fading and everything around them changed. They were no longer at the top of a rock face. The Valley of Flowers had disappeared.

CHAPTER – 12

BELOW FREEZING POINT

Steve and Cheeka were standing in knee-deep snow. The boys turned around in amazement. "Where are we?" asked Cheeka.

"Alaska, I suppose," replied Steve. "And Pinkoo? Where is she?" He looked around and all he could see was an endless landscape of snow! There was no sign of Pinkoo anywhere.

"Pinkoo!" called out Steve. He was so concerned about that delicate butterfly that he did not even realize how poorly clothed he was for the freezing cold. He looked around and called out again. "Pinkoo! Pinkoo, can you hear me?"

"Yes…brrr… I can hear…y-y-you!" came a faint and trembling voice.

"That's Pinkoo's voice, isn't it?" he asked Cheeka, who was shivering with cold.

"I-I..th-th-hink so…" said Cheeka.

"But I can't see her." Steve turned all around, screaming, "Where are you? Pinkoo?"

"H-h-here," came the answer.

Steve looked at his right shoulder where Pinkoo used to sit. But she was not there. "Here? Where, Pinkoo?"

"In your p-p-pocket!" came the feeble answer.

Steve soon covered his pocket with his palm to give Pinkoo some warmth. That's when he realized how cold he was, too. They had to take shelter somewhere, as soon as possible.

"Do you have any idea about this place? Where should we go?" Cheeka asked Steve.

Steve took out the map. It unfolded and floated mid-air. "According to this map, we're somewhere deep inside Alaska," said Steve. "I've never been here before. But I did read about the mountains once. I know that we're at a very high altitude and the oxygen level is low. I've heard that people can faint due to lack of oxygen. And it will get much colder, once the sun sets."

The mention of "sun" reminded Steve that he could take in the sunrays to energize himself. He raised his right palm toward the sun and held Cheeka with his left hand. Soon the rainbow on his palm started to glow and his body became warm. The growing heat in his body passed through his left palm into Cheeka's body. This was a unique experience for Cheeka, and also for Pinkoo, who was growing warm inside Steve's pocket.

"Umm! That feels much better," she said, peeping out. "Well done, Steve! Keep it up!"

"Thank you, dear princess!" smiled Steve. He looked around for a direction to proceed. As far as his eyes could see there was snow. No houses, no humans, not even animals. He turned to Cheeka. "What do you say, Cheeka? Which direction should we take?"

Now that he was warm, Cheeka was more relaxed. He looked at the sun, which was now their only point of reference. "Why don't we start walking in the direction of the sun?"

Steve and Pinkoo agreed.

The trio waded through the knee-deep snow. There was a strange stillness in the air, probably because there were no sounds of birds or animals. Only an occasional howl of the wind would shriek through the silence. The atmosphere was such that even the kids did not talk much among themselves. An unknown land, and an unknown destination; they had no choice but to keep going.

After walking for a distance, they reached some sort of a boundary that was made of blocks of ice. The transparent blocks formed a large circle, in the middle of this nowhere land.

"Stop!" said Cheeka. Pinkoo peeped out of Steve's pocket and looked around.

"What is it?" asked Steve.

"See this circle of ice?" said Cheeka solemnly.

"It looks like a big wall. Are you sure it's a circle?"

"Yes. It's a rare sight, but I know about it. I have heard about it from my masters and seen it in ancient paintings. One gets to see such a sight in the mountain regions only once in a lifetime. It is a sacred circle of meditation. For ages some powerful soul has been meditating here." Cheeka asserted solemnly.

"Here….Where?" asked Steve.

"Inside the circle."

"But I can't see a soul."

"Let me fly and find out," said Pinkoo enthusiastically.

"No...Please!" said Steve. "That's the last thing you should do in this freezing cold. Let's move on."

"I don't think we should cross the sacred circle," said Cheeka.

"Then what do we do?" asked Steve impatiently.

"Go around it."

"It will take us hours to go around this huge circle. And if it gets dark, we'll freeze to death."

"But crossing the sacred circle is dangerous," said Cheeka, visibly scared.

"We are taking a risk, either way. Let's keep going."

Steve clamored over the ice wall. After a moment's hesitation, Cheeka followed him.

The sun was approaching the horizon. The kids realized that though the sun rays kept their bodies warm, breathing was becoming very difficult. The low level of oxygen was making them drowsy. And, as if this was not enough, the air was suddenly filled with a strong pungent odor.

"What's that smell?" asked Steve. There was no reply. "Hey, Cheeka?" Steve asked again.

After a moment's silence, Cheeka spoke slowly. "If what I am guessing is right," he said, "we better be careful!"

"But...why?" Steve asked, feeling very uncomfortable. "Where is this stink coming from?"

"Quite close to us, I feel," replied Cheeka.

"And what is it?" asked Steve, impatiently.

Before Cheeka could reply, Steve tripped on something and fell. He got up and looked at what he'd tripped on. There was something orange sticking out of the snow. Curious, Steve dug out the snow around it. Soon he could see a florescent orange horn-like object sticking out of a hairy surface. The horn was transparent and hollow, and glowed from within. Steve tried to pull it out of the snow, but it was firmly stuck to the hairy surface.

"That's not what we are here for," reminded Cheeka. "And this is not just any other creature."

"Well, if you know what it is, why don't you solve the riddle?" asked Steve.

Before Cheeka could reply, out sprang a large, hairy ear from under the snow. It hit Steve, and the impact was so great he was thrown several meters. Cheeka ran to rescue him, but suddenly another huge ear popped out of the snow. Cheeka tripped over it and came down with a thud. The boys were shocked out of their wits.

Now the earth started trembling. From under the thick snow burst out columns of hot smoke. The smoke had a weird orange color and was so hot that it started melting the freezing snow around it. The tremors grew strong and wild. Steve and Cheeka narrowly escaped being hit by the shooting hot smoke, and they found it difficult to balance on the shaking earth.

"Oh God!" said Steve. "Is it an earthquake?"

"No…its…its…" Cheeka seemed to have lost his voice.

The earth shook violently, and the horns of the creature glowed like fire. It appeared that some intense activity was taking place under the earth. Steve held strongly to Cheeka's hand.

"W-… what's going on, Cheeka?"

"It…It…It's the Yeti king!" shouted Cheeka, struck by panic. "Run, Steve…Run for your life!"

By now Steve was equally aware of the danger. With one hand on his pocket to protect Pinkoo, he ran with all his might. Cheeka followed, shouting, "We should run toward the boundary of ice slabs, at the other end." But running in knee-deep snow was no small task. The boys kept struggling as the tremors grew stronger, making it even more difficult for them. Suddenly, with a thunder that seemed to shake all of Alaska, the boys were thrown apart and the shudders finally stopped. Steve looked back, aghast. From under the thick layers of snow burst out a giant animal, the size of two elephants standing on top of each other. It was like a tremendously huge man whose body was covered with a thick coat of golden fur that glistened in the evening sun, and with two florescent horns glowing atop his head. From under his bushy eyebrows, two eyes glittered like rubies. His long heavy hands extended down all the way to his knees. His body seemed to emanate immense heat, which caused pungent smoke all around him. Steve froze with fear. Cheeka grabbed his hand and dragged him along. "Run…For God's sake…Run, Steve!" shouted Cheeka.

That's when Steve came back to his senses. He ran behind Cheeka as hard as he could. And, as expected, the mighty Yeti chased them. He had been disturbed from centuries of meditation and would severely punish whoever had troubled him.

The boys were no match for the Yeti's speed and strength. They knew they had to somehow cross the ice boundary. But one step of the yeti was more than ten leaps that they could manage. When Steve and Cheeka were just about to reach the boundary, Yeti King was just two steps behind them. He positioned himself to take a huge jump.

The boys leaped over the ice. But instead of landing outside the boundary, they landed on the ice itself. The block started sinking into the snow with their weight. And when the ice had completely receded, before the boys could work out what was happening, they found themselves rolling down a strange tunnel.

The icy walls of the tunnel were slippery and absolutely freezing. As they went deeper into the tunnel, it got worse. The chill was biting into their skin. Breathing was getting more and more difficult. The tunnel took them through multiple twists and turns and tumbles, until they landed on a giant web made of elastic-like strings of snow. Steve thanked God for the web, because if they had slammed into a hard surface at that speed they would have turned into pulp.

The force of their impact bounced them in the web until they came to rest. Then suddenly the web of strings threw them up with a big push. The boys went flying deep through the heart of a huge cave. They saw long icicles hanging from the ceiling of the cave, like ropes. They tried to grab them, but the snow simply melted in their hands. Steve knew they would soon hit against the hard ice on the ground and that would be the end. And they did hit the ground. The boys closed their eyes tightly, imagining that their eyes would never open again. But they realized they'd landed on what felt like rose petals.

Steve took some time to open his eyes, because he thought that he might still be falling. But when he opened his eyes, yet another incredible sight awaited him. What corner of earth was this?

CHAPTER – 13

A HIDDEN WORLD OF SNOW

The surface on which he had landed was made of small white globules of snow that reminded Steve of medicine tablets. They were spread all over the floor and the walls and they also hung from the ceiling.

Steve had still not recovered from the shock of the fall. As he lay buried under thick layers of the tiny snow balls, he was amazed to realize that the snow covering his body kept him warm. He should have been frozen by now, but it was quite the opposite. He also realized that the snow globules were not still. Everything around him was in motion. It was as if he were floating amidst a calm sea. The globules would build up into a wave and pass over his body, almost drowning him. Then they would recede, leaving him floating atop. There was constant movement on the walls and the ceiling as well.

The tiny snow balls on the wall were merging into one another, forming weird figures that appeared to be alive. These abstract figures would come close to each other and then move away, revealing cracks in the snowy wall. Through these cracks, a mystical violet light filled the cave.

When the globules filled a crack, the violet light peeked through the tiny gaps between the snow globules.

As well there were snow globules hanging like stalactites from the ceiling of the cave, swaying like the tentacles of an octopus. They looked porous, and their pores exuded smoke that filled the cave with a misty aura.

Steve was so engrossed in this world of snow globules that he had forgotten about Cheeka and Pinkoo. Suddenly he remembered them and was wracked with fear. He quickly reached for his pocket where he had hidden Pinkoo, but, to his despair, the pocket was empty. Shocked and scared, Steve called out, "Cheeka...Pinkoo!"

His voice echoed from all corners of the cave. But there was no answer. Steve felt uneasy, with the mysterious globules crawling all over his body. He tried to get up and look around for his friends, but he was not getting a footing on the unstable floor.

After some struggle, Steve managed to stand up, knee-deep in the globules. He called out for Cheeka and Pinkoo again but got no response. Amidst the play of violet light and shadows, he looked very carefully, searching for some glimpse of his friends. He felt that he saw something moving, at the center of the cave. Cautiously, he walked in that direction. As he drew nearer, he realized that it was the hand of a kid sinking under the snow globules. Was it Cheeka? Suddenly the sinking hand moved and Steve heard a faint voice. "Help...Please! Somebody...help!"

Steve called out with all his might, "Cheeka! Is that you, Cheeka?"

"Yes, Steve, it's me! Please save me Steve. But listen, don't—"

Before Cheeka could complete his sentence, Steve leapt toward him and soon realized his blunder. He felt his feet sinking as if in quicksand. The snow globules under his feet started swirling. Gradually the whole floor moved and churned like a giant whirlpool, sucking Steve into it.

But he was more concerned about his friend, who was just a couple of feet away from him; Steve didn't realize that he was himself chest-deep inside the icy quicksand. He stretched himself out with all his strength. But the more he struggled, the more he got sucked into the speeding whirlpool. At this point, all he knew was that Cheeka should be saved. And it was the love and concern for his friend that gave him the strength to take one final leap and grab Cheeka's palm. The touch of his friend gave him such a relief that he forgot that he would sink any moment. And that's exactly what happened. He held Cheeka's hand tightly as they sank into the quicksand.

Steve gasped for breath. His body seemed to be entering an infinite hole. Although he still held on to Cheeka's hand, Steve finally felt that the end had come. All his effort, his entire struggle, was going to be futile. With his eyes barely above the quicksand, a breathless Steve felt his vision dwindling. With his blurred vision, he thought he saw a spot of pink fluttering amidst the spotless white globules surrounding his eyes.

The pink spot came close to him and, he heard a voice that lifted his fading spirits. "Steve!" shouted the familiar voice.

"I can't believe this! Pinkoo?" he shouted back, trying to get a better look through the globules that filled his eyes. As he opened his mouth to talk, the globules gushed into his throat and he choked.

"Don't talk, Steve," said Pinkoo, "hold on to this quickly."

Steve saw that with her tiny legs Pinkoo was holding a long tentacle hanging from the ceiling. She heaved the tentacle toward Steve, stretching it like an elastic band. But with every inch of progress that Pinkoo made, she found Steve sinking further away from her. His head was already below the snow. He held his breath because he knew that if he tried to breathe, the globules would get into his mouth and nose and choke him. He could not open his eyes, as the globules scraped against them when he did. He was losing his senses fast. There was just enough energy left in him to hold on to Cheeka's hand and to keep another hand out of the quicksand. Everything seemed to be in vain, and Steve felt his spirit sinking.

Just inches above him, little Pinkoo was using her last bit of strength, her tiny legs trembling, to stretch the tentacle to Steve's fingers. His body was completely submerged in the snow globules, but he was fully aware that he was holding Cheeka with his left hand and his right palm was sticking out of the quicksand. The palm was the only trace of Steve that Pinkoo could see, and it was her last hope. She knew that she could not hold on to the string anymore. She had exhausted all her energy and her tiny wings could not flutter. An inch from Steve's palm, the elasticity of the tentacle had now started pulling her backward. Filled with hopelessness, tears pouring from her eyes, she would have to give up.

That's when Steve's palm started glowing. And out

came the brightest rainbow Pinkoo had seen. It pulled the tentacle toward him. Blinded by the unexpected rainbow, Pinkoo lost her grip on the tentacle and fell down, completely exhausted. As she fell she was sure the tentacle must have bounced back to the roof. In her mind she saw a vivid image of Steve and Cheeka drowning into the globules. She opened her eyes with a jolt, and screamed, "No! This can't be!" And before her eyes she saw the answer to her prayers.

The rainbow rays emanating from Steve's palm acted like a powerful magnet, and the tentacle was following its command. It submissively moved toward him until he had a good grip on it, and as soon as Steve clutched it, the huge whirlpool came to a standstill. The tentacle vibrated as its elasticity yielded to the strong influence of Steve's delicate palm.

Steve knew that if he pulled the tentacle further, it would snap and all efforts would be in vain. So he lightly tugged at the tentacle and leapt out of the globule swamp, pulling Cheeka with him. The tentacle yanked the two kids out like lightning, and they flew toward the ceiling of the cave. But before they could touch the ceiling, the entire cave was filled with a bright violet luminescence. The snow tentacle carrying the boys started gravitating toward the source of that light—a huge opening in the wall. The boys went through the opening and on the other side of the wall they were transported into a world that was beyond anything their minds could comprehend.

They were at least thirty feet above the ground when Steve lost his grip on the tentacle. Even Cheeka slipped from his hand. But although they had been thrown up at great speed, their fall was slow and gentle. In fact, Steve felt like he was floating. It felt as if they were on the moon, where gravity is much weaker.

Steve touched the ground like a feather. The place where he landed was bathed in violet rays. Steve realized that he was actually standing inside a huge crystal ball. Strangely, the walls of the crystal ball, which should have been reflecting the violet rays, seemed blurred. He then realized that the walls were actually rotating at a great speed. It was probably because of this high-speed rotation that the gravitational pull had reduced.

As soon as he thought of the reduced gravitation, he wanted to test it again. So he jumped up with all his might and went as high as ten feet up.

From that height, he could see that the violet rays pervading this huge crystal ball were emerging from a bright spot on one end. Steve caught a glimpse of this source of light and felt something unusual about it. He landed on the ground again and stood for a while, pondering. What was unusual about the violet light source?

Something struck Steve, and he sprang up for another jump. This time he stared right into the light source, even though the rays were blindingly bright. Steve had to strain his eyes to get a better view of what he thought he had glimpsed earlier. After a few jumps, when his eyes got used to the brilliant light, he saw that the source looked like a cobweb of violet rays. A cobweb that was animated and alive! And in the middle of the cobweb was fluttering a colored creature. It was Pinkoo!

"No!" shouted Steve, as he landed on the ground. He soon realized that Cheeka was missing, too. "Why do I have to separate from my friends like this every time?"

In the meantime, Steve felt that he had heard a mumbling sound. He stood silently for a while, trying to listen attentively to any sound, any hint of where Cheeka was. Then he heard it—a very faint and weak "Mmm…mmm…"

"Cheeka!" he shouted. "If you can hear me, please say something!"

"Mmmm…." Was all he could hear.

Steve rushed toward the voice. He reached a partition made of snow globules. The globules were the same kind that he had seen on the other side of the cave, before had landed inside this crystal ball. Where could Cheeka be? Steve had distinctly heard the voice behind him.

"Mmph…"came the sound again.

This time Steve was sure that the voice was coming from behind the wall of snow globules. Steve struck the snow globule partition with his shoulder. Like a house of cards the globules went flying in the air and Steve fell on the other side of the wall. And yes, Cheeka was in front of him. But Steve wasn't happy to see him—at least not the way Cheeka looked at the moment. He was lying down, with hundreds of thin white strings, nailed to the floor by white globules, running all over his body, tying him down. Steve rushed to Cheeka and held out his hand.

"How did this happen to you? Who tied you up like this?"

Cheeka could not utter a word; his mouth was sealed with white strings. There were strings tied across every inch of his body. Every hair on his head was nailed to the floor. His ears were tied. His nose was pressed so hard by the queer thin white strings that he could hardly breathe. Even his eyebrows were nailed to the floor with those strings.

He could barely open his eyes. In deep agony he looked at Steve as if he was trying to say something. Steve could not bear to see his friend in such pain.

How did this happen? They had been apart for only a few minutes. Who tied him up? There was not a soul around.

Steve realized that there was no point in wasting time over these questions. He had to rescue his friend, without further delay. The strings were very thin and Steve thought that he could break them easily. But there were so many, and they were tied so tightly that Steve could not decide where to begin!

He managed to grip a bunch of strings tied to Cheeka's chest. He was about to pull it when Cheeka mumbled something. Steve looked at him. Cheeka was trying hard to say something, but his mouth was all tied up. All Steve could understand from his expression was pain, and maybe some kind of warning. But what was Cheeka trying to warn him about? Steve had no time to think. He only knew that he had to free Cheeka from this mysterious captivity, and then, Pinkoo from that weird violet web. There was no time to lose. Hurriedly Steve pulled hard at the thin white strings, hoping they would snap instantly. But the strings turned out to be much stronger than he had imagined. He pulled again, harder this time. But things got worse. The harder he pulled, the harder the strings tightened on Cheeka's body.

"Ummph....!" Cheeka let out a painful groan. Now Steve realized what Cheeka was trying to say earlier. If he pulled at the strings any harder, it would dig into Cheeka's skin.

Steve let go of the strings and wondered what he should

do next. He did not want to leave his friend in this condition. On the other hand, there was Pinkoo caught in the mysterious web. As he stood there, totally lost, he was unaware of the intense activity behind him. Then he heard Cheeka's pained voice. Steve turned around to see…..

Thousands of ice globules from the floor of the cave, were fast advancing toward him. Although they looked like sweet little globules earlier, they appeared formidable right then.

Once again he heard Cheeka's muffled shriek. He was frantically trying to say something to Steve. Soon he felt the globules climbing up his legs. He stamped his feet to free himself, they stuck on. He bent down, took a handful of the globules, and smashed them into a lump. His hands worked fast and soon his legs were free. Now his only option was to run away from them. So he ran toward the source of light, hoping to reach the violet web and free Pinkoo. But due to the weak gravity, his feet could not move him forward very quickly. The globules were fast catching up with him. If only the power of gravity was normal!

He had taken a few strides when a strange sound behind him made him look back. The globules that he had crushed into lumps were changing shape, turning into tiny human figures that looked like soldiers. Little soldiers made of ice! They looked like knights and warriors from some ancient period, fully equipped with armor, helmets, and weapons. In awe, Steve watched as the ice warriors multiplied. More globules came together and formed many more of those tiny creatures.

One of the warriors looked stronger than the others and came forward to take the lead. He took out his spear and held it high above his shoulder. In a faint voice, which must have been loud enough for his size, he let out a sound. Steve could hear the voice but did not understand the alien language. But he knew that the leader's voice was communicating an order. And immediately, the entire battalion, which numbered in hundreds now, followed the leader and raised their spears. Steve couldn't help but find it amusing.

His amusement turned into shock when he heard the leader blurting out a mighty war cry. The leader threw a spear. It would have struck Steve's nose if he hadn't jumped back. It fell near his toe, a thin white string attached to the end. The string wrapped itself around Steve's foot. Steve lifted his foot, thinking that the thin string would easily break. But he was wrong. In fact, it seemed to pull on him tighter. Before he could think of another move, all the soldiers followed their leader and threw spears at Steve. Tiny strings attached to all those spears tied themselves around his legs. Steve fell down on his face, with a thud.

Now he knew what had happened to poor Cheeka. Lying on his chest, he thought hard about all the possible ways of getting out of the situation. Suddenly, he remembered that he had been given a small knife by the residents of the Gompa, before he left for the expedition. He quickly searched and found it in his back pocket. But the moment he tried to cut the thin strings, the blade of the knife became cold. The strings were made of snow! The knife was covered with ice and Steve had to let go of it.

The warriors picked up globules that magically turned into spears. Within moments, more spears were hurled at Steve. Every part of his body was tied and pinned to the ground. Steve somehow managed to keep his head turned to one side so he could see ahead of him. He felt so handicapped and dejected, lying on the floor unable to move. He was reminded of *Gulliver's Travels*, in which the main character was also held captive by tiny people.

But these were no little people, these were strange creatures made of ice. Steve saw the creatures morph back into ice globules as they scattered away. With them, the violet light around him started moving away. The spinning walls of the crystal sphere slowed down and came to a halt. With this, the gravitational pull increased and Steve's body felt heavier. He felt exhausted, weak, and very lonely. Lying helplessly, he looked back in retrospect.....

CHAPTER – 14

HOPING AGAINST HOPE

Steve reviewed the chain of events that had stormed through his life within a period of barely a week, since he was sent off from his home in New York. He was filled with thoughts of his friends back in the Holy Family orphanage…his home, which was now thousands of miles away. Though life was tough there and he had faced many hardships, the orphanage was where he had grown up. He thought of the bakery where he used to bake cakes, pastries, and buns. It was just about a week back when he was baking dry fruits buns for Christmas. 'Oh my God!' he thought. Christmas must be just around the corner. And this will be the first time in all these years that I will not be with my friends to celebrate Christmas. Steve had lost track of the days and did not know when Christmas would arrive. 'Who knows whether people in this part of the world have even heard of Christmas?' he thought, as his heart sank. He was not sure whether he and his friends would survive this situation.

Lying flat on his face, he felt helpless and insecure. He prayed to God and called out to Shom for help. And, as if

God had heard his prayers, the walls of the cave started rotating again. As their speed grew, his body felt lighter and he could breathe more easily. Gradually, the violet rays grew brighter and Steve felt that the source of the rays was coming toward him. The violet web was growing bigger. It was obviously advancing toward him, and he hoped it would not bring him further trouble.

His fear transformed into hope when he saw a faint vision of colored wings fluttering. Could it be?

Yes, it was Pinkoo! Steve heaved a sigh of relief, thanking God she was alive. But he decided to lie low so that no more trouble came to her.

Pinkoo was still caught in the web of rays. But she did not appear to be hurt. Steve was finding it difficult to look at the brilliant light around Pinkoo, but he did not want to keep his eyes off her. As Pinkoo and the violet aura came closer to him, Steve felt that the source of the light was not something abstract, as it had appeared from a distance. It was actually the figure of a creature. And what an unusual creature it was! Standing just about a foot tall, with a body that appeared to be made of snow. Fluffy snow that had a shape, but not a definite one. It was like a piece of cloud that had taken a human sort of form. This snow-white figure had a head that was larger than the rest of his body. He wore a long and flowing beard that reached up to his knees. The face was chubby and had a cute, button-like nose.

The only thing on his body that had color was a pair of gleaming blue eyes that shone brightly from under flowing, white eyebrows. In sharp contrast to his soft snowy body was the armor that he wore. This glistening armor was made of hard, sharp-edged ice. The strong armor gave him a robust look, and the shining ice helmet resting on two big round ears made him look truly like the leader of the battalion of ice soldiers.

As the leader walked toward him, Steve noticed two more peculiar features. One, he was not walking, but floating a few inches above the ground. Second, the bright violet rays were actually emitting from the center of his forehead. These violet rays had woven a web in which Pinkoo was captive. The figure came close to Steve, and his blue eyes looked deep into Steve's. Steve felt a series of ice-cold waves travel through his body.

In the midst of all these distractions, Steve's attention was fixed on his friend. "Are you okay, Pinkoo?" asked Steve softly.

Pinkoo looked straight at him, but could not talk.

"Say something, little one," said Steve.

Pinkoo just kept looking back at him without uttering a word. She appeared to be under a hypnotic spell.

"She can't talk," informed a deep, rumbling voice. Steve looked around to see who was talking. There was no one but the small creature in front of him. He must be an alien, from some other galaxy, thought Steve.

"No, I am not an alien," said the creature. "We all belong to earth."

"Are you...are you reading my thoughts?" asked Steve.

"Yes. I can read your thought as simply as I tell you mine," he said.

Steve was reminded of his grandmaster Shom, who also communicated with his thoughts. But he wondered how another creature could have such an incredible power which he thought only his master possessed.

"If you aren't an alien, how come you're so different? You don't seem like anything that comes from earth."

"We belong to the human race," said the creature. "But we are far more advanced than you. Our bodies do not perish like yours. We belong to this sacred ice land and live a life frozen in time. There is no beginning or end to our lives. We keep changing our form, depending on the situation."

"So your present situation demanded that you recruit your entire battalion to capture two unarmed boys and a tiny butterfly? How chivalrous was that? " said Steve, who was quite cheesed off by now.

"This is not a battalion," said the creature. "We are the Viola tribe. For centuries we have been deputized to protect the earth from evil forces. You three are intruders into our world. This is why you have been held captive."

"We didn't mean to intrude," said Steve. "We had no clue about this secret world. It was an accident that brought us here." Steve went on to describe how they'd tripped on the Yeti and in a frantic attempt to escape they slid into the tunnel.

The leader of the Violas listened to him attentively. After thinking for a while, he talked again without moving his lips. "One thing is clear...you are not lying." Steve watched the creature silently as he went on. "But I wonder how you are still alive!"

Though the creature was more or less without facial features, Steve could clearly see the change in his expression; his blue eyes shone brightly, looking directly into Steve's eyes. "Not many humans have seen the Yeti. And those who have seen him are not alive. The one you saw is, in fact, the king of the Yetis...the supreme, powerful leader of the Yeti clan. He has acquired many powers through intense meditation.

"For centuries, the Yetis have been trying to rule this region. We have fought them and protected our land, because we know that if they overpower us, they will they will rule this region. There are many secrets hidden here. These secrets have been protected by the inhabitants of these mountains for centuries. They have trusted us with these secrets, and now it is our duty to protect them.

"But King Yeti refused to give up. So he went underground to perform a meditation that would make him invincible. For years he was buried deep in the snow, surrounded and protected by the powerful meditation circle. How did you enter the Forbidden Circle? Not to mention how you distracted him from his decades-old meditation. It is difficult to believe you are still alive. There must be some powerful force protecting you."

"You're right," said Steve. "We are protected by our grandmaster at all times."

"Your grandmaster?" asked the creature. "Who is your grandmaster?"

"My grandmaster belongs to the sacred land of India. He is the leader of a Gompa—a Buddhist monastery at the foothills of the Himalayas," said Steve.

"I request that you tell me your master's name," said the creature, looking curiously at Steve.

"We are not supposed to share our master's name," said Steve, loud and clear.

"It's important for all of us," the creature insisted.

"I can't," was Steve's defiant answer.

"I implore you to tell me your master's name," said the

creature. "If he is the grandmaster from a Gompa in the Himalayas, I must know his name. This might change everything right now."

"Shom!" was Steve's short reply.

At the mention of Shom's name, the creature took a few hurried steps backwards. He stood there looking deep into the eyes of Steve, as if searching for something within them.

Steve watched the creature closely. He felt like those glittering blue eyes were swimming in a few drops of water. And a drop of water trickled down his snowy check. 'Is he weeping?' thought Steve. 'But why should he weep?'

The creature replied to his thoughts. "What have I done?" The Viola leader's eyes were filled with remorse. "How could I make such a big mistake?" Then he waved his hand in the air. Within seconds, hundreds of ice warriors came and stood before him. The creature waved both hands and seemed to speak to the warriors in some kind of sign language. The next moment the soldiers turned into tiny snow globules and rolled over to cover the bodies of Steve and Cheeka. As if by magic, both the boys were freed from their bondage. They ran and hugged each other. Soon the violet web rays disappeared for a moment and Pinkoo was free. She flew and hugged the nose of both her friends. All three were united at last. The creature watched them silently. Then he floated over to them.

"Brother," he addressed Steve. Steve was taken aback.

"Why do you call me brother now?" Steve asked rather curtly.

"Do not misunderstand me, brother," said the creature remorsefully. "We are like brothers because we are disciples of the same grandmaster. If we exist today, it is because of our master's protective blessing and guidance. He has been guiding me and my clan for years. I thank God that the truth about you and our grandmaster was revealed to me before it was too late. If I only knew this, you would never have gone through this trouble. We are indeed very sorry, brother." As he said this, the entire clan of warriors walked up to Steve and his friends and laid their weapons at their feet.

"Oh, no, no… please! You don't need to do this. I know you had to capture us because we were trespassing. If we hadn't come to this land, bumped into the Yeti king, and tripped and fallen into your cave, none of this would have happened," Steve said with a sad heart.

"Oh yes, I should have thought of that earlier. I did not guess that you could have landed here by accident," said the leader of the clan. "But tell me brother, how did you get into this trouble?"

"It's a long story," he said. "The past week has been full of incredible incidents. It feels like several years have passed within a few days."

"Your eyes tell me the story of long pain and struggle," said the creature. "But please tell me what brought you to this land. Was it our grandmaster's desire? Is he all right?"

"He's in trouble," said a teary-eyed Steve. The thought of the deep anguish and pain that his master must be suffering filled him with sadness.

"What has happened? Please tell me everything, in detail," said the creature, looking visibly concerned.

Steve narrated all the incidents that led them to Alaska. An uneasy silence took over the place. The horror unleashed by Koraka in the peaceful land of the Gompa filled the creature's eyes with tears. "Oh, my good Lord!" he sighed. "Why did this have to happen to our master? And innocent kids like you and your friends had to go through such pain!"

The creature and his clan listened to Steve in rapt attention as he went on to explain that he was here in pursuit of the first of the seven paintings—the Violet painting. That's when Pinkoo butted in with, "We've got to find the violet painting and then the six remaining paintings. Can you please help us?"

"It is my duty and the duty of our Viola clan to do everything we can for you. We are called the Viola tribe because we are born of the violet light. Violet is our lifeline, Violet is our power. The Violet painting would be most secure in our land."

"We have a map that can show us the location of the painting," said Cheeka.

"But...I think we lost it during our accidental fall into this cave," said Steve, feeling unsure.

Pinkoo was shocked to hear this and wondered how they would continue with their expedition.

"Nothing gets lost in Viola land," said the leader. "My soldiers found it and have taken good care of it."

He pointed his fingers toward the floor and gestured, as if communicating to the space around him. Out of thin air emerged a floating, violet-colored symbol. Then the violet rays emitting from his finger tips pushed the symbol onto the floor. Before the awestruck eyes of the kids, the map came out of the floor and attached itself to the violet symbol. The creature made another gesture with his finger and the symbol disappeared, leaving the map floating in front of them. The map was fresh and alive as ever.

Steve walked to the map to take a closer look. The land, the sea, the desert, the rivers—everything was still clearly animated. However, the mountain range of Alaska looked hazy. The mountain seemed to be covered with thick snow and mist all over. Strangely, the violet spot that had shown the location of the violet painting was not visible now. But somewhere in the center of the mountains there was an open space that appeared like a valley. Right in the middle of this valley was a shining golden spot. This was a new addition to the map which Steve could not understand. "Do you recognize the golden spot?" he asked Cheeka.

"No. I can't recollect having seen this spot on the map."

"It may be something that is related to these people," whispered Pinkoo into Steve's ear.

"You are right, little one," said the leader, giving Pinkoo a shock.

"Oh God!" whispered Pinkoo again. "How did he?"

"Shh!" said Steve. "He knows everyone's minds. He reads our thoughts."

"But he doesn't know my name," said Pinkoo. "He called me 'little one' just now!"

"You are right again, little one!" said the creature, smiling. "I can read your thoughts. But if you don't tell me your name, how will I know?"

"You have given me and my friends enough trouble," thought Pinkoo. "Why should I give away my name so easily? And, by the way, why haven't you told us your name?"

"I am really very sorry, little one, for all the trouble you have gone through. And everyone here calls me Grand-brother. Should I call you Little Sister?"

Pinkoo stared at Grand-brother in amazement. "You really can read our thoughts," she said. "I thought only our grandmaster had this power."

"It is through his blessings and training that I have acquired this power, little one," said Grand-brother. "Now tell me, do I call you Little Sister, or by some other name?"

"Well, I am Pinkoo, and these are my friends, Steve and Cheeka," said Pinkoo.

"We are confused, Grand-brother," said Steve who was still puzzled by the new addition to the map. "Do you know what this golden spot is on our map? It wasn't there before."

Grand-brother looked at the map. He closed his eyes and started meditating. Gradually a spot in the center of his forehead started to emit a violet beam, scanning the map. When the scanning beam reached the golden spot, a golden star appeared there.

Grand-brother opened his eyes and smiled. "You are lucky, Steve. This is the auspicious Golden Star, which appears only once every year. And this is that time of the year. This great star will lead you to your painting. But it is not as easy as it sounds.

"The great Golden Star is visible only for a few minutes. You have to grab it as soon as it appears. I say 'grab it' because I have a feeling that you are not the only person who is looking for it. There are other greedy hands that want to own it. Don't forget the Yeti clan and their king. The Golden Star could lead them to the Violet painting, and then to the Creatures of the Rainbow!

"These paintings have come out of their secure abode in the Gompa for the first time in history," Grand-brother went on. "Like the greedy and evil Koraka, many others will be eyeing those powerful paintings. So, Steve, my brother, now you know what lies ahead of you."

"All I know is that I am on a mission given to me by my grandmaster. And with the help of my friends Cheeka and Pinkoo, I will fulfill it!" said Steve with determination.

"And our grandmaster is with us always," reminded Cheeka. "He has been protecting us and will take care of us until we accomplish our task."

"My grandmaster has given me the responsibility of my friends, and I will never let them down!" added innocent Pinkoo.

To this Grand-brother added, "Consider us a part of your mission. Our grandmaster is in trouble, and we will do everything possible to help you."

"Without your help we will not be able to do anything, Grand-brother," said Steve. "Please guide us."

"Of course, we are all one in this mission!" said Grand-brother. "Now, the first thing to consider is where the Golden Star will appear. It is far from here, and the terrain is rough. It will not be easy to reach the place. Secondly, we have less than twenty-four hours to get there. The Golden Star will appear at midnight tomorrow, and you will have just a few minutes to grab it. So forget sleep, forget hunger. We have to get started right away!"

Grand-brother waved his fingers in the air and produced another floating violet symbol. All the tiny soldiers present in the cave gestured and produced many more such violet symbols. Within moments, hundreds of symbols were floating across the cave. As if in response, thousands of snow globules crawled toward Steve, Cheeka, and Pinkoo and attached to their bodies.

Grand-brother could tell the kids were startled. "Don't worry, you will not be hurt. We have to venture into the bitter cold. They are preparing you for that."

Within a few moments, Steve's, Cheeka's, and Pinkoo's bodies were totally covered with snow globules. Then the globules receded down their bodies, revealing warm fur coats in their wake.

"That's better," said Grand-brother. He turned toward the Viola clan and addressed them. "Friends, we need to set out on the most important mission of our lives. Let us make it absolutely clear in our minds that this is not a mere journey. It's a mission. It involves our grandmaster and three friends who are very precious to us. I want all of you to be aware that the path to the valley of the Golden Star is not only difficult but is filled with danger at every step. We might be encountering natural calamities or man-made obstructions. But let this not deter us from our mission. The Golden Star has to be in the hands of our friends at any cost."

Grand-brother then turned to Steve. "Brother Steve, we pledge all our support to you and your friends. But there are certain things that you need to remember. The valley of the Golden Star has a circle in its center. This is called the 'Forbidden Circle.' This is the rarest piece of land on earth, unknown to the rest of humanity. It is because of this circle that the earth remains in its orbit."

Steve, Cheeka, and Pinkoo listened in amazement, but were not able to completely comprehend what he said.

"Let this not distract you, my friends," continued Grand-brother. "I had to mention the Forbidden Circle because you have to take extreme caution before entering it. This is an area where the gravitational pull is stronger than anywhere else. It is at this spot that the gravitational force of all the planets and the sun is focused. Anyone who steps into this area will get pulled by tremendous force to the center of the earth. His body weight will increase many times and taking a single step can drain all his energy. If a person remains within the circle too long, he will be pulled to the heart of the earth and will perish."

This was a frightening thought. Steve noticed Cheeka and Pinkoo staring at him. But right now Steve wanted to think about the task in hand. "What about the Golden Star?"

"I am coming to that," said Grand-brother. "The Golden Star will appear at midnight, exactly at the center of the Forbidden Circle. This is the only time when the gravitational power of this area becomes normal—that is, similar to the pull of gravity in other places. That will be your chance to enter the circle. But this chance will last for just a few minutes. The Golden Star will disappear as fast as it will appear. Once it disappears, the gravitational power inside the Forbidden Circle will increase tremendously, and everyone inside the circle will be crushed by it—except us, the soldiers of the Viola tribe. We have been gifted the power of turning into snow balls. We will merge into the snow and come out of the circle."

Grand-brother turned to his soldiers. "It's time for us to make preparations to come out of our cave and start our journey toward the valley."

All the ice soldiers gathered near their leader. He signaled to them, and they made a circle around Steve and his friends. He closed his eyes and folded his hands in a gesture of meditation. As he meditated, the violet gem on his forehead started to glow again. Gradually he raised both his hands toward the ceiling.

"Brother...!" Steve could hear Grand-brother speaking to him through his thoughts. "Please hold each other tightly, and do not let go until I ask you to."

"Yes, Grand-brother," said Steve, and he held Cheeka's hand. Pinkoo took refuge in his pocket.

Everyone looked at the ceiling. The violet rays emitting out of Grand-brother's hands spread like thick violet clouds on the ceiling of the cave. Gradually, the clouds started revolving. Out of nowhere a strong wind gushed into the cave and started circulating. The wind moved in the direction of the clouds, adding to their speed. Now the walls of the cave also started rotating, in sync with the movement of the wind and clouds. The circular movement inside the cave gained tremendous momentum. It all created a tornado of sorts. Steve had heard of twisters, and here was one right in front of his eyes. Such was the power of the wind that he felt breathless, and the whirring mist was blurring his vision. He could hardly see anything. Even Cheeka seemed to disappear in front of his eyes. He clutched Cheeka's hand tightly. Soon his feet were swept off the ground and he realized that it was not due to the powerful wind but to the lack of gravity inside the cave. In fact, it did not appear to be a cave anymore. The rotating walls and the ceiling made the structure appear like a huge space ship. Steve and Cheeka were now floating midair.

"Hey, Cheeka!" said Steve. "Are you feeling the same as me?"

"I am floating!" shouted Cheeka in excitement. "And I see you are floating, too!"

"But I am not floating," said Pinkoo peeking out of Steve's pocket, "let me try."

"Absolutely not!" screamed Steve. "You'll get sucked up by this tornado. Just stay put!" He pushed her back into his pocket.

"How selfish!" grumbled Pinkoo. "Why should boys have all the fun?"

The huge structure lifted from inside the earth above ground. While Steve and Cheeka were struggling to stay together, the little ice soldiers were firmly stuck to snow on the floor.

Steve saw Cheeka fumbling for something inside his fur coat. "What are you looking for?"

"It's the map," replied Cheeka. "I am not sure where I put it."

"This is not the time for it, Cheeka. Let things settle down. I'm sure everything is in place," said Steve.

But Cheeka was worried he'd lost the map. After groping for some time, he found something and drew it out immediately. And in this hurry he committed the biggest mistake. The strong wind snatched the map away from his hand. It flew at lightning speed and got sucked into the twister. Cheeka panicked and lunged toward the map, and before Steve could realize what was happening, he had lost his grip on Cheeka. Cheeka dived toward the twister and got swallowed by it, as did Steve's screams, "No, Cheeka... No!"

Cheeka disappeared inside the twister. Grand-brother warned against following him. "Have patience, brother! We will save him." But nothing could stop Steve from acting now. Without a second thought, he plunged into the twister and was lost out of sight.

Inside the twister was a volcano of energy. This was the tremendous energy that was buoying up the cave from its domain underground. Flying at the speed of sound, Steve maintained his senses. He looked around. There was no sign of Cheeka. The energy created by the tremendous movement of the wind and the clouds emitted sparks of lightning inside the twister. Anything hit by the flash of fire would be charred in an instant. Steve was using all his energy to keep afloat and save himself from the lightning. Suddenly Cheeka appeared before him, then disappeared in a flash. In that fraction of a second, Steve could make out that Cheeka was unconscious. Amidst that chaos he focused all his energies to save the situation. He looked up and discovered that at the top end of the tornado, the land was opening up and a sharp streak of sunlight was filtering through it. Steve stretched out his hand and used all his energies to focus on his rainbow power. In no time powerful rainbow rays burst out of his palm and pervaded over the powerful twister. And then another miracle happened.

A new tornado grew inside the twister and started rotating in the opposite direction. A powerful gust of energy rose upward and blasted a hole in the huge ceiling of the cave. At an unbelievable speed, both twisters swept through the hole, taking the boys along with them and throwing them outside the cave, into the open land. With dwindling vision,

Steve saw Cheeka being flung out with him. And then it was all black.

CHAPTER – 15
JOURNEY TO THE GOLDEN STAR

Bright daylight glistened on the white snow. Steve tried to adjust his eyes to the light and also to see through the thick fog that blurred everything in front of him. He could make out the faint outline of Cheeka's body lying beside him.

When he moved closer, Steve was reassured to see Cheeka's tired smile. He quickly felt his pocket, and, as if on cue, Pinkoo peeped out and said, "I must say you guys have become extremely irresponsible. Imagine, grown-ups like you, jumping into twisters and getting into trouble. What a rollercoaster ride that was. I am still giddy."

"OK, calm down, little one. I get scared when you are angry," said Grand-brother with a smile. Pinkoo gave him a dirty look. Grand-brother and his group surrounded the kids. Cheeka looked around, his eyes searching for something.

"Is this what you're looking for?" asked Grand-brother, showing the map. Cheeka smiled faintly.

"You need to stop worrying. Worry is in your mind. It is a negative feeling which makes a situation into a problem.

The situation remains as it is, but worry compels you to make choices that worsen the situation. And that's exactly what you did, my friends," said Grand-brother. "I understand and appreciate your concern. But be assured, brother, that the Viola tribe shall always protect you and do everything that you need to accomplish your mission."

Steve and his friends listened to Grand-brother attentively. It was the lesson of a lifetime for them.

"You're right, Grand-brother," said Steve. "We've learned our lesson the hard way." He turned to Cheeka and said, "Let's get on with the map."

Cheeka looked at the map. A narrow path leading to the Golden Star was faintly visible. However, there was a dark black spot on top of the mountain, and it kept blinking. "This black spot was not there earlier. What could it be, and why is it blinking?"

"I think your map is indicating some unforeseen danger. It's a warning of some sort. Right now it would be difficult to guess what it is. We will know for sure only when we reach the mountains," said Grand-brother, now appearing a bit concerned.

He turned to his soldiers and addressed them. "This map indicates a hidden path leading to the west, to the Golden Star. We first need to find that path."

Grand-brother looked at the snow that spread for miles ahead of him. There was no sign of a path. Steve and Cheeka looked around but could see nothing more than vast expanse of snow. The ice soldiers stood still, waiting for orders from Grand-brother. An uneasy silence fell over the place, broken only by the occasional noise of the sharp winds blowing.

"Hey look! I can clearly see the route through the map!" Pinkoo said in an exciting voice.

Everyone jerked at the sudden interjection.

"Where are you, Pinkoo?" asked Steve.

"Up here," said Pinkoo. Everyone looked up and saw Pinkoo floating along with the map.

"You are smarter than I thought, little one," said Grand-brother. "How did you manage to take the map up there?"

"I asked it to help me and it just came along," said Pinkoo, smiling. "Hey, Steve!" she continued. "I think you know how to use this map. You can find the path for us."

Steve understood what she was trying to say. He raised his right hand toward the sun. As the sunrays touched his hand, a beautiful rainbow emerged from his palm and passed into the map. The map was immediately vibrant with colors that spread across its length and breadth. Somewhere on the other end of the map, the seven colors re-converged into the dazzling ray of the sun. This strong beam hit the ground below. The entire group watched in amazement as the brilliant light coming out of the map paved its way through the snow. As it dashed ahead, the snow around instantly melted and gave way, revealing an idyllic path leading to the mountain.

There were smiles all around, as Pinkoo flew down with the map. Steve and Cheeka gave her a loving hug. Grand-brother patted her on her cute little wing. "You have done a great job! We are proud of you."

Pinkoo pulled up the collar of her new feather coat, put on the golden crown presented by the queen of butterflies, and looked around with pride.

"Well, friends, no time to waste; let's march on."

Grand-brother took the lead and the party followed. They moved on with hope in their hearts...unaware of careful eyes that watched every move from the sky.

Although his evil master was trapped in a mirror maze, Koraka's bat had not lost sight of Steve. It was now time for this loyal messenger to report the latest. The bat flew to a barren thorny bush. Hanging upside down on a branch, he transmitted high-frequency sound waves that crossed the planet and penetrated all objects between it and the mirror maze inside the Gompa.

The ultrasonic waves touched Koraka's staff. The diamond on the tip of the staff started to glow. Koraka opened his eyes with a jolt. His ears turned toward the ultrasonic sound, and like a transmitter he received the bat's message. "Master... Master!"

"Stop panicking, you fool!" an irritated Koraka communicated through supersonic sound waves emitting from the diamond of his staff.

"Pardon me, Master, but they are moving west toward the mountains. Their magic map has made an easy path for them. If all goes right, they will reach the valley of the Golden Star before long." The bat's voice was quivering as he said this.

"It's a big 'if,' my dear disciple. Remember, a big 'if' can make any action questionable. A big 'if' can make any journey impossible. And I am the impossible factor in their journey. Do you think a handful of kids and a bunch of pygmies can achieve what I—the greatest Koraka—cannot achieve? I shall crush them before they reach the top of the mountains. Are you ready?"

"Yes, my lord. Command me."

"I know a person who will dig their watery graves. He is the gurgling witch doctor, Goya, an old friend. Go to him, and he will take care of everything."

"But where can I find him, Master?"

"Simple, my evil boy," chuckled Koraka. "Look for the Red Lotus in the mystical pond, on the eastern foothills of the mountains. Now go!"

On the western route, where the party had made good progress, Grand-brother suddenly stopped. The others, who were behind him, came to a halt.

"What is it, Grand-brother?" inquired Steve.

Grand-brother kept quiet and closed his eyes. It looked like he was concentrating on something. His fluffy, cloud-like fur contracted as he stood still, trying to feel some-thing. After a while he broke his silence. "An activity in the east makes me uneasy," he said. "I receive messages of destruction."

The whole group watched in silence as Grand-brother rose from the ground and floated in air.

"Our grandmaster warns us of evil forces that may dis-rupt our mission." Grand-brother raised both his hands as he spoke. "Friends, let everyone understand that we are here for a great cause. We are on a mission of service to hu-manity, to save our planet. We are on the path of God and no one...*no one* can stop us. Remain united; remain close to each other, no matter what the eventuality. May God be with all of us! Let's move now!"

The group moved on with new dedication in their hearts. But little did they know about the scale of danger lurking behind them.

At the eastern end, a black bat was flying restlessly, in search of the Red Lotus. In the huge expanse of snow that spread for miles, a pond was beyond imagination. After a while, he got exhausted and perched himself upside down on a thorny branch.

'Where on earth can I find a pond in the middle of this frozen land?' he wondered hopelessly. Just then, his attention was drawn to a mirror-like spot glistening at the foot of the mountain.

'Is it...?' He flew toward the shining spot. But as he approached, the shining spot disappeared. He was sure he had seen the spot and was flying in the right direction. Disappointed, he looked around and soon saw the glistening spot in another area. He flew toward it. But before he could reach the spot, it disappeared and appeared in another area. This sequence of events repeated itself several times.

Exhausted and frustrated, the bat went back to his thorny branch. Hanging upside down, he closed his eyes and thought, why is this happening to me? Is it some mystical experience?

"No! It's a punishment!" It was Koraka's stern voice.

"Master!" the bat opened his eyes in shock. "Why this punishment? What have I done?"

"How could you start on a mission without worshiping me?" commanded Koraka.

"I am indeed very sorry, my Lord," said the bat remorsefully.

"Then say, 'Long live Koraka!" commanded Koraka.

"L…Long Live Koraka!" shouted the bat in fear and awe.

"Repeat!" came Koraka's command again.

"Long live Koraka!" repeated the bat.

"Again," ordered Koraka.

"Long…live…Koraka!" said the bat trembling.

"Now open your eyes," commanded Koraka.

The bat opened his eyes to see that right below the branch where he was hanging was a bright red lotus, in the middle of a small pond. The deep blue water of the pond was shimmering in the bright sunlight. 'How could the water remain liquid in the middle of a land covered with snow?' wondered the bat.

"My lord! You are great!" said an overwhelmed bat. "Only you could create such an illusion. The Red Lotus is right below this branch. What do I do now?"

"Ha-ha-ha! Illusions and miracles are a part of Koraka's life," said the evil man with pride. "Now what are you waiting for, stupid? Go and snatch the lotus."

The bat hesitated for a while. He knew that there was some black mystery in every illusion that Koraka created.

"What are you waiting for?" boomed Koraka's voice.

"Well, nothing actually…" said the nervous bat.

"Then go for it, you fool," shouted Koraka.

The bat had no choice but to obey his master. He dived at the Red Lotus. Quite famished by now, he could not resist digging his fangs into the heart of the Red Lotus. As he dug his blood-sucking fangs he thought, Never mind that this is not blood. As least I will enjoy the sweet nectar of the Red Lotus. The bat sucked hard at the lotus's center and suddenly stopped. 'I can't believe this!' he thought. He sucked harder.

"Long live my master!" he cried. "How can I ever thank you? This is pure blood! You knew how thirsty I was!"

Hearing no response, the bat pinched himself to ensure that he wasn't dreaming. How can a lotus possibly have blood inside? He went on sucking greedily.

What he didn't realize was that as he sucked the blood, the color of the Red Lotus was fading and its petals were growing larger. Gradually, the blood-red lotus became white. Its enlarged petals now looked like the ears of an elephant.

The bat sucked and sucked until the last drop of blood was gone. The contented bat then looked around in amazement, feeling a bit drowsy. Now the lotus was absolutely snow white and ten times larger than its original size. "Hey! Wasn't this lotus red in color?" he said to himself.

"You are right."

The shocked bat looked around to see where the answer came from. But he could spot no one.

"It's me, the lotus you are sitting on," said the lotus.

"You can talk, too!" said the bat, now a little alarmed. "How did you turn white and so big?"

"Because you sucked all my blood," said the lotus.

"But I have not heard of a lotus with blood instead of nectar," said the bat rather nervously.

"Well, what were you suckling, you greedy little creature?" asked the lotus.

"It tasted like blood," said the bat meekly.

"It was blood. But not my blood," said the lotus, quite matter-of-factly.

"Not your blood?" asked the bat in fear.

"You see, you're not the only one who was lured by my lovely red color!" said the lotus, sounding rather proud of her cunning intentions. "My color has proven to be a fatal attraction for many a creature. They end up here, and I get their last drops of blood."

"Do you mean that you are…?" said the confused bat.

"That's right, you greedy bat! I am a blood-sucking lotus!" With this last statement, the huge petals of the lotus began closing in on the bat.

The bat struggled to fly, but his feet were stuck to the sticky surface of the lotus. He could not move. The bat screamed, "Hey! Hold on; this is not fair!" as the large petals shut over him.

"And you think it was fair when you drank from my petals?" resorted the lotus.

"Well, eh…I was hungry…and…thirsty…" The bat's reasoning was clearly not working on the lotus.

"Well, I am thirsty all the time. Ha-ha-ha!" The eerie laughter echoed within the petals that tightened over the bat. Soon, small sharp needles came out of the petals.

The bat was overcome with such immense fear that he could only manage a squeak. "Are you trying to kill me?"

"No, I am trying to play soccer with you…Heh – heh!" chuckled the lotus.

"This is no time for jokes," said the trembling bat. "You can't kill me. I am on a mission."

"Most animals make this excuse before they die. Do you have a last wish, eh?" said the disinterested lotus.

"Yes! I want to meet Goya—the gurgling witch doctor," the bat said hurriedly.

Suddenly the grip of the petals loosened. "What did you say?"

"I want to meet Goya, the gurgling witch doctor," repeated the bat.

"Who told you about him?" asked the Red Lotus, a bit bewildered.

"My master Koraka"

"Why did you not tell this before?"

"You did not give me a chance," said the bat meekly.

"OK, OK! Let's not argue," said the lotus as he reopened his petals. The needles were pulled back inside. "Don't worry now. I won't harm you. Just come with me." The Red Lotus covered the bat with her petals and dived into the pond. She swam deep into the blue waters under the snow. After swimming for a while, she came up to the surface and opened her petals.

The bat looked around. It was a dome made of ice, partly transparent, partly opaque. Sunlight filtered through the transparent part, revealing the shape of the place. "What spooky place is this?" whispered the bat to himself. Skulls of different shape and size hung from the ceiling. Lizards, cockroaches, and other insects had made their homes inside them. A lizard jumped to eat a cockroach, but slipped off and fell into the water. Surprisingly, its body was charred and turned to ash in a few minutes. That was when the bat realized that the Red Lotus was not floating on water. It was probably some kind of acid. The liquid bubbled and popped. Huge blocks of ice floated on this boiling surface, as well as skeletons of animals and humans.

The bat was lost in these sights when the Red Lotus screamed, "What are you staring at? You have come to meet our master, Goya, haven't you?"

"Yes. Oh yes! I forgot…" The bat was still dizzy.

"So call him," the Red Lotus interjected.

"Yes, of course." The bat gathered all his courage and called out "Goya! Goya!"

Thud! Down came a petal on the bat's head. "Are you out of your mind?" said the annoyed lotus. "He is our master. The king of this land! Address him with respect!"

"Very sorry!" said the bat. Then he shouted out again, "Your Highness! Master of all the gurgling witch doctors! King of the land of gurgling acid! I beseechingly request you to make your kind appearance and help your humble servant."

Soon large bubbles surfaced at the center of the acid pond. The bubbles grew in number and size, becoming a fountain. The sound of the gurgling liquid grew so loud that it echoed all around the dome. The bubbles were followed by thick gray smoke. Then from under the bubbling acid emerged a figure. The bat tried to see, but the thick smoke blurred his vision. How would the strange creature look? How would he talk? How would he react? All he could make out was that the mysterious creature was huge and fat. He mustered all his courage and finally spoke. "Are you Goya?"

"GURGLE...!" With a large gurgling sound the creature spat a thick liquid fireball toward the bat.

As he dodged the fireball, the bat realized his mistake and said, "Am I the fortunate creature to see the grand appearance of His Majesty, King of the land of gurgling acid, Lord Goya?"

"Gurgle – gurgle...You have still not seen me," came a deep but hollow voice from behind the smoke. "So why lie?"

"Sorry, your Heaviness...I mean...Your Highness!" said the bat, now more nervous than before, "but I am keen to see you."

"Gurgle – gurgle – gurgle...(SPIT)!" The creature spat another ball of liquid fire and immediately the smoke cleared. From behind the smoke appeared a horrid-looking creature with the face of a fat man and the body of a frog. Each of his eyes had two eyeballs that rotated in opposite directions. The face was greased with oil. Thick drops of perspiration seemed to be a permanent feature on the forehead. The mouth was broad and extended from one ear to the other. A green, slithering tongue lolled out of its mouth permanently. The body was like a bulky toad with a fat yellow stomach, all of it covered in shiny green scales resembling those of a fish. Behind him followed a thin, thorny tail that moved constantly across the back of his body.

Goya did not seem to care about the bat's presence. His four eyeballs rolled around as if searching for something. Then he found it. His tongue sprang out of his mouth, stretched out more than twenty meters, and caught a giant spider on the ceiling. The tongue jerked back into his mouth, and Goya swallowed the huge spider in one gulp.

"Gurgle – gurgle," said Goya, smacking his lips. "Oh! I was starving."

The bat looked at him fearfully. "Yes, sir. In fact, you deserve much more than this." He didn't know why he was saying all this. Probably he was trying to overcome his nervousness.

"So, Blacky…(gurgle)…what brings you here?" said Goya.

"I am in trouble. My grandmaster, Koraka, said only you could help me," said the bat, hoping the evil creature would understand him.

"You are my friend Koraka's disciple? (Gurgle) You should have told me earlier. I was about to (gurgle – gurgle) have you for lunch. You are a well-fed bat, Blacky! I like you." Goya rolled his green tongue over his lips and pushed one left-over hairy leg of the spider into his mouth.

"Hee hee…" The bat tried his best to smile, while his knees trembled. "My Lord! The Gurgling King. We don't have much time in hand. We need your help!"

"Well, what is the matter?" asked Goya.

The bat narrated the entire story as precisely as he could, finally adding, "They are advancing fast. We have to stop them before they cross the mountains."

"Gurgle – gurgle…Ha ha…ha ha. Gurgle – gurgle…heh heh!" Goya gurgled and laughed and croaked for a long time. "Why are you so worried, Blackie? This is a trifle for Goya. They will never be able to cross *my* mountain. If they try, they will perish!"

CHAPTER — 16

THE IMPENDING DANGER

Unaware of Goya's intentions, Grand-brother steadily led his team to the foothills of the mountain. Steve looked up at the majestic mountain covered with snow and wondered how he would be able to climb it. He looked at Cheeka, who smiled back at him.

"I've never climbed a mountain, have you?" he asked Cheeka.

"Some hills," said Cheeka, "but not such a huge mountain. And we have no equipment to help us."

"Wish I could fly like you, Pinkoo!" said Steve.

"But this doesn't look too easy for me either," said Pinkoo.

"Why do you worry when Grand-brother is with you?" said Grand-brother, smiling at them. He signaled to his tribe. "Friends, now begins the difficult part of our journey. The only way we can reach the top is by becoming one with the snow. Our brothers do not have the means to climb. So we will become their steps. Are you with me?"

"Always, Grand-brother," came the chorus.

Grand-brother smiled and made a violet symbol in the

air. With the wind, the symbol passed over every member of the group. Steve and Cheeka felt as if tiny violet crystals were raining over them. Pinkoo peeped out, caught a couple of crystals, and hid them inside Steve's pocket. The crystals had a calming effect on everyone. It filled the kids with confidence and courage.

"This will protect you from all dangers," said Grandbrother. Then, turning to Steve, he said, "And remember, the path you have chosen is God's gift to you. You are on this mission because God feels you are special. So have faith, and face everything that comes your way. God will always protect you." Then, like a war cry, he called out, "Let's go!"

While Steve and Cheeka were still wondering how to start the climb, the ice soldiers turned into snow globules once again. The globules then merged together to form a block of ice.

"That's your first step," said Grand-brother to Steve and Cheeka. "Please step on it."

As Steve and Cheeka climbed on the block, another block formed above it. One by one, block by block, the boys started climbing the mountain. While it seemed that things were finally working out, no one had the slightest idea of what was being conspired behind their backs.

Inside his den, Goya was preparing a large-scale assault. The bat watched in awe. With his long tongue, Goya plucked out five skulls from the ceiling: an owl's skull that had a family of cockroaches inside it, a pig's skull that was the hideout for a rat, a frog's skull that had frog eggs laid inside it, a lizard's skull nesting a beehive, and, finally, a human skull that had a live human heart throbbing inside.

Having collected the skulls and their animals and insect residents, Goya dumped them all into an ancient copper cauldron. The old, rusted pot looked exquisite. It had images of all the planets of the solar system engraved on it, with the sun in the center. Goya put both his hands into the cauldron and crushed the contents. As he made a paste of the skull and animal parts, the rust on the cauldron disappeared and the copper began to shimmer like it was new. Goya then took a deep breath and held it. A couple of minutes passed, but Goya did not exhale. The bat watched as Goya's face gradually turned red and his nostrils spread wide. Even then Goya did not release his breath. Smoke started coming out of his nostrils and ears. Goya continued to hold his breath. His face swelled, turned crimson, and looked like it was about to burst. Finally, Goya spat a big lump of molten fireball into the cauldron.

The bat shrank to the corner of a petal on the lotus, watching the frightful sight. The moment the liquid fire ball fell into the cauldron, it mixed with the pulp inside. That spurred a sudden burst of activity within the cauldron. On the exterior of the pot, the planets and sun came alive and started moving in their orbits. Within the cauldron, the contents started to boil. It appeared as if a fountain of fire was erupting from the base of the pot. The concoction grew. Intermittently, steaming tentacles of the boiling liquid reached out from the mouth of the cauldron. The planets on its surface revolved at a tremendous pace around the sun, which shined like a ball of fire. The liquid inside it turned to an angry red color, much like the lava of a volcano. At this point the pot started shaking. Goya watched all this with pride. In his excitement, his body turned orange as he grew bigger in size. His eyeballs—all four of them—turned red.

He raised his hands high up into the air and shouted with arrogance, "Oh shadows of death (gurgle...), blood and blight (gurgle...gurgle...), I call on thee to assist me!

He spat another ball of liquid fire into the pot, and instantly a volcano erupted from inside. Red hot lava leaped out, and the moment it touched the acid in the pond, it began evaporating and forming thick black clouds.

The bat crouched into his wings, peeping out to see the drama unfold. The ice on the dome started to melt with the heat of the activity, and the cave began to tremble.

Steve and his friends had reached halfway up the mountain, climbing step by step on the ice blocks created by the Viola tribe. At this height, the temperatures had touched below zero degrees. It had started to snow and sharp winds were blowing, making their journey difficult. Grand-brother paused for a while and asked Cheeka for the map.

While Grand-brother was studying the map, Steve noticed his expression becoming graver. "Is everything OK?" he asked.

"This black spot is bothering me," said Grand-brother.

Steve saw the map. The black spot that they had seen earlier had grown bigger.

"What does this mean?" asked Cheeka.

Grand-brother was visibly worried. "Well, let it not stop us. We will face it when it shows up. Let's move on."

The party continued with their journey.

Suddenly, Cheeka slipped on a step and Steve held his hand.

"What happened?" asked Steve.

"I don't know," said Cheeka. "It felt like the ice block shook."

"He is right," said Grand-brother. "I can also feel tremors in the mountain. This is not a good sign. These tremors are unnatural. We should hurry up. But remember, come what may, we stay together."

Goya's den resembled an impending disaster waiting to be unleashed. The thick acid clouds had caused cracks in the ice dome. Goya looked gleefully satisfied with his achievement.

"Yes! (Gurgle – gurgle) Yes!" he shouted. "Now is the right time to strike! I order you acid clouds to burst open from this cage and devastate everything on the western end of these mountains. Remember, not even an ant should be spared. GO!"

He spat another huge fireball at the ice ceiling. The molten fireball burst opens the already cracked ceiling, making way for the clouds to go through. Like a volcano, the smoke gushed through the hole and spread across the sky.

The blast was felt all along the mountain range. Grand-brother, Steve, Cheeka, Pinkoo, and all the brave soldiers of the Viola tribe stood still. They were just about fifty meters from the summit. The explosion in the den had shattered the ice blocks making their staircase.

Cheeka and Steve were standing on separate ice blocks, both of which had almost broken into two pieces. Both of them stood still, not daring to move. Cheeka, standing on a higher block, gathered his courage and extended his hand down to Steve.

"Come on, hold my hand and jump onto my block, Steve. Yours might break any moment," said Cheeka.

Steve held Cheeka's hand and was about to jump when there was another blast. With the blast, the cracked step on which Steve was standing gave way. The tiny globules forming the ice block went tumbling down. The globules were trying to unite and form into soldiers, but the speed at which they were falling made it impossible. A few meters down were huge rocks that would mean their end. At the last second, bright violet rays pierced through them all and held them together. It was Grand-brother. Floating mid-air, he was emitting life-saving rays through all his fingers. With their violet lifeline propping them up, the globules rolled toward each other, merging together and forming ice soldiers. "Thank you, Master! You saved our lives," they said in gratitude.

"I am bound by my duty, my brave soldiers," said Grand-brother. "We shall always be together. Now let's march."

Grand-brother and the ice soldiers quickly rushed to the spot where they had left Steve and his friends. They found that the boys had been saved by other soldiers, who had managed to hold on in spite of the blast. Steve and Cheeka were standing on a big block of ice.

"Is everything alright?" asked Grand-brother.

"We're safe for now," said Steve, "but things don't seem to be all right." He pointed east at the monstrous black cloud moving toward them. No one had ever seen such a horrifying cloud.

It covered half the sky and seemed to hold some boiling liquid that was emitting smoke all around. The cloud was so huge and heavy that it could not rise high. It remained close to the lower range of the mountains, waiting to burst open.

"This is no ordinary cloud. It is not nature's creation. Whoever has created this had evil intentions. And we are the target," said Grand-brother.

Goya's den was full of jubilation. An unending stream of lava flowed out of the copper cauldron and merged into the acid, forming an endless stream of acid clouds. The clouds were forming so fast that the acid pond was almost empty. The bat was now hiding behind a rock. Goya was dancing with joy, singing out a tune…..

"Ha! gurgle – gurgle – gurgle…
Ho! gurgle – gurgle – gurgle…
'Death' is a beautiful thing…
That's why I like to sing!"
He roared with laughter and continued…..
"Go evil clouds, and rain – rain – rain;
Do the 'Rain dance of Death'!
Again and again…..
Go – Go – GO!"

Grand-brother was sure that whatever those clouds held was disastrous for them. "If these clouds were to rain here, no one would survive. We need to reach the foothills on the other side of the mountain right away. Or maybe we can find shelter. But we need to do it quickly."

"Where will we find a shelter in this wilderness!" said Steve, desperate by now.

"I have found one!" a jubilant little voice said. Pinkoo signaled from a cave higher up the mountain. The boys' faces brightened up.

"There seems to be enough room in the cave for everyone," said Pinkoo, smiling.

"You are our savior, as always!" said Cheeka with tears of joy.

"But it's quite far," said Steve. "Climbing on blocks takes time. Do we have time to get there?"

"There are other ways to the cave," said Grand-brother, and turned to his soldiers. "Friends, listen to me carefully. Divide yourselves into two groups. Arrange yourselves into one large rectangle."

As the ice warriors followed their leader's command. Satisfied, Grand-brother said, "Now, brothers Steve and Cheeka, lie down on them."

"But....How could we? Won't they...?" Steve was not able to complete his sentence.

"We have no time to lose," said Grand-brother in urgency. "Trust me, and do as I say."

Each boy climbed on to one squad of soldiers. Grand-brother transported himself to the cave. From there he extended his hands toward them. Hundreds of violet strings came out of his fingers. "Hold on to the strings," instructed Grand-brother.

The ice soldiers tugged at the strings, which were as

strong as ropes. Carrying Steve and Cheeka on their heads, they pulled their way up the mountain. Cheeka looked in horror at the fast-approaching acid cloud.

"Don't look up. Soldiers, pull!" shouted Grand-brother.

The soldiers clambered with all their strength. At one end were hundreds of soldiers carrying Steve and Cheeka's weight, and at the other end was Grand-brother, all alone. Still, the party managed to move swiftly.

But the clouds appeared to be approaching faster. The ground trembled beneath it. Some soldiers lost their balance and Steve slipped from his position. But they quickly regained their formation.

Inside the den, Goya was in his ugliest best. His body had turned red and he had grown into a huge monster. Throwing his arms in the air he shouted, "Rise, rise, my friends from hell, (gurgle…), get your sharpest arrows, (gurgle…gurgle…), pierce the acid clouds and explode it. In your hands now, I put my biggest dream!"

Lightning flashed across the sky. The thunder that followed shook the mountains. Grand-brother closed his eyes in meditation and was drawing all his strength from the universe to pull the strings. The brave ice soldiers were using all their might to move forward. They were making good progress and looked like they would reach the cave in time. Suddenly a large flash of lightning cut through the violet strings, shaking Grand-brother from his meditation. The boys and the soldiers stood stunned! They were hardly ten meters away from the cave. The clouds were about to rain acid, and their ominous rumbling tore the mountains apart.

The ice soldiers lost their grip and began to slip downward.

CHAPTER – 17

LETHAL CLOUDS STRIKE

T his is not good, O God!" said Grand-brother, trying not to give up hope. "Friends, only our grandmaster can save us now."

Steve felt Grand-brother's helplessness. He knew now it was up to him to save the situation.

Steve looked up. A faint beam of sunlight was visible, but would soon be hidden behind the clouds. Without wasting a moment, he lifted his right palm toward the sun, absorbed all its energies, and emitted a bright rainbow toward the cave. Grand-brother and all the ice soldiers watched in amazement as the rainbow spread inside the cave and buoyed the team.

Although the team was moving toward the cave at great speed, the menacing acid cloud was moving faster. The mountain range continued to tremble under the thunder and lightning.

When they were just about two meters from the cave, the ugly clouds completely covered the sun and Steve's rainbow disappeared. Thunder rumbled through the mountains and created an avalanche that tumbled toward the group.

Thousands of sparks of lightning pierced the acid clouds. They threatened to burst any moment, charring away everything. Tremendous gusty winds seemed to blow everything away.

"Don't give up, for God's sake!" said Grand-brother, at the top of his voice. "You are just a few steps away from your goal! Just believe in yourself and see yourself achieving what you want! Use all your strength and climb up! I know you can do it!" Such was the power of the wind and freezing snowfall that Grand-brother's fluffy soft body seemed to disintegrate. But the brave-hearted leader firmly stood his ground. The boys were totally exhausted by then. With the sun disappearing behind the menacing black cloud Steve seemed to be powerless. How he wished for a glimpse of the sun so his rainbow power could save everyone. Cheeka felt the freezing wind piercing through his warm clothes and entering his bones. But he held to his friend with all his guts. The brave soldiers had started to deform under the tremendous pressure of snow and wind. But they were not ready to give up, and they made one last attempt. They lifted the boys on their shoulders and took them up to the cave, using every bit of their dwindling energy.

As the last handful of soldiers entered the cave, an mammoth explosion of lightning pierced right through the cloud and burst it into pieces. And all hell was let loose. Millions of gallons of concentrated acid gushed onto the mountain.

Grand-brother saw that about a dozen ice soldiers were stuck under a rock. He rushed to them, covered them with his violet rays, and carried them with all his might toward the cave. Struggling against all odds, they were about to get back into the cave when the avalanche rumbled over their cave's opening. There was a total blackout inside the cave. The survivors in the cave stood still. The last thing they needed was to lose Grand-brother.

The entire mountain range was wracked with devastation. Avalanches were let loose. One avalanche followed the other, one after another after another...Hundreds of avalanches, pouring down like monsters. They destroyed every tree and shattered boulders, pieces of which were hurled into the valley at tremendous speed.

The entrance to the cave was blocked with ice. It was pitch dark inside. Nobody knew who had managed to get in or how many of them were safe right now.

The noise outside was deafening. Even if someone were to talk aloud, no one would hear him.

An inferno of acid was running down the mountain slopes. The fiery heat of the acid battled the freezing cold of the snow. Amidst harrowing vapors and hissing sounds, miles of snow instantaneously began to boil. The next moment, boiling water mixed with fuming acid gushed down the mountain, destroying everything along the way. Temperatures that, seconds ago were below freezing, had now reached boiling point.

The boiling acid devoured all vegetation and life in the forest at the foothills. What was beautiful, fragrant, and pleasant had turned ugly, pungent, and desolated. Goya's act of malice had killed thousands of innocent plants, animals, birds, and insects, which had nothing to do with the architect of this destruction.

Mother Nature silently stood watching the carnage, triggered by a mad creature. Was there any justice on this earth given to such mindless destruction? Stranded hopelessly in the dark, this thought was overpowering in the hearts of every survivor in the cave.

At the other end, in his den, Goya—the evil, gurgling witch doctor—was thumping his chest victoriously. What a firework he had created! Little did he know that his evil creation was about to be stopped and brought to justice

The lava erupting from inside the copper vessel kept on flowing. The acid had totally vaporized and the huge pond was dry. Now the lava started filling the pond. Goya was too busy celebrating to notice the impending danger. The bat quietly watched the molten fire fill up the pond steadily. He sheepishly began with, "Excuse me, my Lord…"

"Yes, Blackie…(gurgle – gurgle)…So finally you open your mouth (gurgle)!" And with his signature arrogance, Goya continued, "Afraid, are you? Ha ha…(gurgle – gurgle)…Ha ha ha ha! Now you have some idea about the power of Goya, eh? I am the destructor!" he screamed madly. "Every little creature on those mountains has been destroyed! (gurgle – gurgle) Not even a fly can…" He stopped as he saw a fly struggling to come out of a cobweb. He shot out his long, green tongue and quickly devoured it.

"Slurp! (gurgle – gurgle) So what was I saying? Ah, yes! (gurgle – gurgle)…not even a fly is left alive. Mission accomplished! Are you happy?" He turned toward the bat, his eyeballs rotating with excitement.

"Very happy…most obliged, sir," said the bat nervously.

"But, my lord, the…" He was distracted again by the rate at which the level of boiling lava was increasing inside the pond. It looked like the pond would overflow any moment, and the liquid fire would burn the whole place down. He was also terrified by the thought that if the map was destroyed along with the boys, he would have no way of finding paintings. And in that case, his master Koraka would strangle him to death.

"What were you saying, Blackie? What is left to say now? (gurgle – gurgle) You selfish bat!" shouted Goya. "I have done so much for you! What are you going to do for me in return, eh?"

"What can a small, useless bat do for you, my Lord?" said the trembling bat.

"You are small, Blackie… but not useless. Hmm…aren't you…(gurgle – gurgle)…well fed? How can you be useless? Eh?" said Goya, looking at him greedily. "You are so very useful to me right now…(gurgle – gurgle)…All I need is a nice juicy meal! After such hard work, am I not hungry? Eh…Hee Hee!"

"W-W-What are you saying…Your heaviness…I…I mean…Your…high-highness?" said the bat, dying a hundred deaths.

"You have heard me right, you nitwit!" said Goya, waving his tongue. "I have given my sweat and breath for you. Now…(gurgle – gurgle)…I want my pound of flesh." Goya sprang his tongue at the bat, which was on alert by then. The bat managed to dodge Goya's lethal tongue.

"Don't you dare run away from me…you…you insignificant little creature! I will…(gurgle – gurgle)…gulp you before you know it!" said Goya, as he lashed his tongue furiously at the bat.

But the bat was not waiting to hear his gurgling curses. He flew higher and farther with all his might.

Goya jumped at him without thinking of the consequence. Luckily for the bat, Goya narrowly missed him.

"Blow!" shouted Goya as he came down. He looked at the surface under him and realized what a grave mistake he had committed. Just below him was the pond filled with boiling lava. And...Splash! He was submerged.

The bat heard the echoes of deathly shrieks. As half of his body turned into ash, the gurgling witch doctor shouted, more in shock than in agony, "Aaaarrgh! Gurgle... Gurgle! BETRAYAL!" His twenty-meter-long tongue tried to whip the bat again, but missed narrowly. Even as Goya was dying, he yelled, "I am the king of all I survey! I will not die alone!" He swayed his lethal tongue all around the dome, catching every skull, skeleton, animal, bird, and insect, putting it all into his large mouth. With so many objects, dead and alive, in his mouth, he could not chew any more. He could not breathe. His face became red and then crimson, and finally, with a huge blast, it burst into pieces. All that remained of him was his long green tongue, which slowly disappeared into the pond of lava.

Goya had paid for his evil deeds. His evil intensions and destructive powers managed to devastate every life in the mountains, but they could not touch a handful of noble beings, which were on a divine journey.

The mountains were burning outside. But it was cold and

dark inside the cave. The noise had settled down and there was silence and calm inside.

"Is anybody around? Please say something. I'm scared," Pinkoo said in a feeble voice. In response to Pinkoo's plea, a violet ray emerged from a corner and spread all over the cave. The ray was emitting from Grand-brother's forehead. It revealed all the faces inside.

"Thank the Lord! Everyone is here—Steve, Cheeka, Grand-brother...and all our friends!" said Pinkoo as she rushed and hugged Steve and Cheeka.

"We are so happy to see you, little one!" said Steve, kissing her wings.

"Grand-brother, it's only because of you that we've been saved. Thank you...thank you from all of us!" said Cheeka.

"Not at all, my brother," said a teary-eyed Grand-brother. "I have always believed that when you are on a mission of goodness, no evil can touch you. God saved us. But we are still not out of danger. It's cold in here, but you have no idea how hot it is out there. Look at the entrance of the cave."

Everyone turned to see that the entrance was covered with a thick wall of solid ice. Grand-brother went up to the entrance and touched the ice. The opaque wall became transparent, revealing the scene outside. Everything was on fire—the mountains, the trees, the animals, everything. The land that had been covered with deep snow now had not a drop of water on it. Never in the history of humankind had the land of Alaska ever made such a pitiable sight. Everyone had tears in their eyes.

"Our beautiful land has gone forever," said a small ice soldier, in tears.

"The birds will not sing anymore!" said another.

"Where will we butterflies get our nectar?" said Pinkoo tearfully.

Steve and Cheeka were speechless.

"How will our Viola tribe survive, Grand-brother?" asked a soldier. "We will melt and die in that heat!"

Grand-brother was listening to everyone calmly. Finally he broke his silence. "Nature is God's creation," he said, "and the creator is always bigger than the destroyer. Nature is meant to heal itself. Haven't you seen trees lose all their leaves and become bare in autumn? But then comes spring, and new leaves grow on the same branches. Flowers bloom again and the birds sing. Nothing is permanent. So if an evil force has destroyed nature and life, it will revive on its own. Change is the law of the universe. And some of us, like Brother Steve here, bring about the change.

"Come, let us join hands and form a circle of Love."

The Viola soldiers formed a tight circle inside the cave. Grand-brother then asked Steve to stand in the middle. "We will now pray to the Almighty," spoke Grand-brother. "We will join our good energies together and send it out to the Universe, and we will ask God to heal nature and life around."

Grand-brother held Steve's hand and closed his eyes. Everyone held each other's hand and stood in silent meditation. After a while, a deep violet halo formed above Grand-brother's head. Gradually the halo grew in size and reached every member standing in the circle. This energized everyone, and formed a halo above each one. All the violet halos came together and formed a violet mist that rose up. The violet mist went through the walls and the ceiling of the cave and spread into the sky. In the presence of the violet mist, all the smoke and dark clouds started disappearing. The calm violet mist covered the sky and soon started raining tiny violet crystals.

The crystals had a magical effect. The fires died. Everything that was burning cooled down. There was calmness all around.

The violet crystals turned into snow. The snowing grew heavier, and within minutes the mountain range was covered with snow again.

Finally, the bright sun peeped out of the clouds. A small beam of sunlight entered the cave through the transparent wall of ice. "That's for you," said Grand-brother to Steve.

Steve put his right palm before the ray. A magnificent rainbow emitted from his palm and spread over the land.

Steve watched in wonder, unable to believe that he was party to that unimaginable miracle. All the birds, animals, and insects came back to life. Birds started chirping, animals ran around, and the beautiful valley was filled again with the fragrance of wild flowers.

The magical intention of love had transformed everything. Creation had won over destruction.

The group opened their eyes. They were filled with joy to see their beloved earth regain its original beauty.

"Congratulations!" said Grand-brother, smiling at everyone. "See how easily nature heals itself! We've only sped it up a bit. And now...it's time for us to resume our journey." Grand-brother went up to the ice wall and touched it with his finger. The ice melted, and Grand-brother led his team toward the summit of the mountain.

By the time they reached it, the sun was about to set. It

cast its orange glow over the valley, the new-fallen snow now shining like gold. Surrounded from all sides by beautiful mountains, the circular valley looked magical. As Steve stood there marveling at the beautiful sight, Cheeka nudged him and pointed toward the center of the valley.

Amidst snow covered land, there was a large barren circle. Nothing grew on it. Nothing seemed to even touch it. And although the entire region was covered with snow, there was no trace of it inside that circle.

"Yes, that is the circle of the Golden Star," said Grand-brother. "See, nothing and no one can enter it. Not even snow or rain. No plant grows there. Anyone entering the circle gets pulled into the heart of the earth and never comes out. Such is the gravitational pull of that area."

The sun had set and it was getting dark. Cold winds started blowing, and visibility was poor. Steve wondered how they would climb down the mountain. Soon night would fall, and visibility would be even worse. He remembered that they had taken a whole day to climb the mountain. There were just a few hours left before midnight. How would they complete their journey in time?

Reading his thoughts, Grand-brother said, "Yes, we have little time in hand. And I've not yet worked out how you will travel down. Our warriors are made of snow. We can easily slide down the ice. But you..." Grand-brother stopped there.

"It's impossible to climb down this huge mountain in the dark of night," said Cheeka, disappointed.

"Don't get disheartened so easily, brother Cheeka," said Grand-brother. "Haven't you heard that saying—Quitters never win..."

"And winners never quit!" Pinkoo completed the phrase proudly.

"That's right, little one!" said Grand-brother with a smile. "You shall always be a winner."

Beaming with pride, Pinkoo looked expectantly at Steve and Cheeka. "We too are proud of you, madam!" both chorused, sulking.

"Don't worry boys," said Pinkoo. "Grand-brother has helped us through worse than this! I'm sure he'll work out a way."

"Thank you, little one!" Grand-brother looked at Steve and Cheeka, who were still sulking.

It was dark by now, and the moon had started rising behind the mountains. Grand-brother faced his soldiers and made a symbol in the air. The beautiful violet symbol lit up the place. The ice warriors understood the message and stood in rows. They raised their hands, and Grand-brother floated in the air and touched their fingers, moving from soldier to soldier. Their fingers lit up like torches. With their finger raised up in the air, they made two rows that moved from the top of the mountain to the base. Steve and his friends marveled at the sight. From where they stood it looked like an airstrip, inviting planes down for a safe landing.

A small group of soldiers waited near the kids. Grand-brother, who was still floating in air, signaled at this group. They turned into globules, and formed a big block of ice that looked like a sled. Then Grand-brother turned to the boys. "Your vehicle is ready, my friends." Steve looked up at him in amazement. "Yes, brother," said Grand-brother. "Just step on it."

Steve and Cheeka climbed on the ice block and immediately it started moving. Grand-brother moved ahead of the block as it started sliding down the mountain. Traveling through the path lit by the soldiers, the block of ice caught great speed. Steve and Cheeka were thrilled. Pinkoo peeped out of his pocket and shouted, "Yippee! This is the most thrilling roller-coaster ride in the world!"

The ice sled jumped through the ups and downs, tilted and twisted at the sudden turns, and even turned somersaults in the air, until it finally came safely to rest at the base of the mountain. The kids were dazed.

"Wow!" said Steve.

"That was surreal!" followed Cheeka.

"Can we do that again?" was Pinkoo's request. Everyone had a hearty laugh.

Finally, when the children recovered from their excitement, Grand-brother spoke, "Thank the Lord that we made it fast. We still have quite a bit of a distance to cover. The moon will be our guide."

A lovely full moon had spread its light all over the valley. The sky was filled with stars that looked so bright that Steve felt he could stretch his hand and catch them. Grand-brother and all the ice warriors glowed in a violet hue. Everything around was so peaceful. Surprisingly, there were no sounds around. Not a bird, not even an insect. It seemed as if no one inhabited the place. As the party moved on in silence, Steve felt a slight tremor in the ground. He thought it was his imagination. A few steps ahead...and suddenly Steve turned behind to discover that some ricks were coming down the mountain. The rocks formed a pile at the foot of the mountain and everything was silent again.

"Stop!" said Grand-brother.

As everyone stopped and looked at each other, Steve confirmed, "Did you feel it, too?"

"Yes," said Grand-brother. "We all felt the earth rumble. And then out of nowhere the rocks came rumbling down" He looked around with his powerful violet ray, but nothing could be seen. He paused for a while and said, "This part of our journey may seem easy, but this is also the part that needs utmost caution. I urge everyone to stay together and take every step with care."

"I am scared!" said little Pinkoo, before ducking back into Steve's pocket.

"Don't worry, everything will be fine," assured Steve, although he was himself uneasy.

"I don't like the smell of this place," said Cheeka, sniffing around. "There is something in the air."

"I can feel that, too," said Steve. "But let's just keep going. We must reach our destination before midnight."

They continued quietly. The moon was shining brighter and things were clearer. But the silence was chilling. The barren circle was getting closer.

They kept moving slowly and cautiously until they reached the spot where the snow cover ended. Steve looked straight ahead at the vast expanse. What a creation of God, he marveled.

As the group stood there in silence, it started snowing. They had all experienced snowfalls before, but this was different. Snow settled on the ground all around, but the snow that fell inside the circle disappeared. The circle of the Golden Star remained stoically unaffected. Though Steve and his friends had heard about this phenomenon from Grand brother, this sight was unnerving.

Cheeka came closer to Steve and quietly held his hand. Steve knew that his friend was as apprehensive as himself. He remained close to Cheeka as they waited silently for midnight. Gradually, the snowing slowed down and stopped. The sky cleared. Steve and his friends looked up to see the moon right on top of them. It shone brighter than ever, and its beam shone straight down at the center of the circle.

CHAPTER — 18

REACHING FOR THE STAR

"I think the time has come to welcome the Golden Star," said Grand-brother. "No matter what happens, no one will enter the circle before I say so. My brave Viola warriors, you will stand exactly around the border of the circle. The moment you see the first glimpse of the Golden Star, throw your snow strings across the circle and weave a net as fast as you can. Remember to leave a passage, though, for Steve and his friends." He then turned to Steve. "Listen to me carefully. Wait for my signal, and don't put a single step inside the circle before I ask you to. And when I say so, run with all your strength toward the Golden Star.

"Don't forget that it will stay for just a few minutes. Catch it and don't let go, no matter what! Remember: if you lose the Golden Star, you will never come out of this circle." Grand-brother sounded solemn.

Steve listened to Grand-brother very attentively. Although he said affirmatively, "I will do exactly as you say," he was visibly nervous.

"I am sure you will succeed," assured Grand-brother. He then concentrated on the center of the circle. The ice warriors had queued up around the circle and were ready to weave the net. There was pin-drop silence. Everyone waited for the historic moment with bated breath.

Finally, it happened. First the moon started to grow in size. Cheeka whispered, "Look at the stars!" They were also growing bigger. "The celestial bodies are coming closer to earth," explained Grand-brother.

What an awe-inspiring sight it was! The moon looked like a huge, round, hot-air balloon and the stars like tennis balls. The whole valley was flooded with their light. And in that light, from under the earth, appeared a beautiful red rose. Its petals bloomed and the sweetest fragrance spread all over. One after the other, the petals unfolded and the red rose grew bigger.

Pinkoo was completely mesmerized by the flower. "What a beautiful rose! I have never seen such a big flower!" Instinctively, the butterfly in her flew toward it and into the Forbidden Circle. Grand-brother cried in vain, "Wait, little one! Wait!"

In an instant, Pinkoo fell on the barren ground and started to flutter and shiver.

"Pinkoo!" shouted Steve and was about to step inside the circle, when Grand-brother pulled him back. Steve helplessly watched Pinkoo tremble and loose her strength. "H-...H-el...Help..." Pinkoo's faint voice reached them all.

"Wait, brother!" pleaded Grand-brother with Steve.

"Just a few seconds..."

And, in all its glory, out came the Golden Star!

"Now...Go...!" shouted Grand-brother, and Steve rushed toward Pinkoo, not caring about the Golden Star.

He picked up little Pinkoo in his palm. She had stopped trembling.

"You crazy girl!" said Steve, lovingly. "Are you all right?"

"Y-Y-Yes…" said Pinkoo, very weakly. "I am…s-s-sorry, Steve."

"I'm just happy to see you alive, my dear!" said Steve.

Steve was putting Pinkoo in his pocket to keep her warm when he heard Cheeka screaming. "Steve! The Golden Star!"

"Run, brother! Run!" shouted Grand-brother. "You have very little time left!"

Steve was jolted out of his oblivion. He looked up. Straight ahead of him was the Golden Star, emerging in all its brilliance from within the earth. Without wasting a moment, he ran for it. Cheeka was close at heel. As they ran, they realized that the Golden Star was attached to something that was emerging behind it. It looked to Steve that it might be a tree. Soon the tree looked familiar. He ran faster, because the tree was coming out very fast and the golden star was rising higher. By the time he reached the tree, most of it was out of the ground. Suddenly, Steve realized what it was and stopped.

Cheeka almost bumped into him. "What happened Steve? Why did you stop? What's wrong?"

Steve was rooted to the ground, mouth wide open, and was staring at the tree.

"Hello!" said Cheeka, loudly so that Steve would get back to his senses. "We are running against time!"

"Don't you see, Cheeka?" said Steve, still lost in the

tree. "It's a Christmas Tree! It's CHRISTMAS, my friend..." shouted Steve. "It's C-H-R-I-S-T-M-A-S!"

Christmas! What he had been missing recently was here! Christmas! For which he was preparing buns with his friends in the orphanage. The Holy Family orphanage, his home in New York, in his own country...America, from which he was thrown out, for no fault of his own. His mind held on to the Christmas of his country that he had left behind. Everything flashed before his eyes. He had given up hope of celebrating Christmas ever again, but God had blessed him with this sight. And what a glorious Christmas tree it was! The largest Christmas tree he had seen in his life, beautifully decorated with festoons and bells, which glittered like jewels. What an unexpected gift this was. With tears of joy Steve, said to himself, "Merry Christmas!"

"Christmas?" said Pinkoo peeping out of his pocket.

"Yes, my dear! Merry Christmas!" said Steve, jubilantly. "MERRY CHRISTMAS, everybody!"

"Merry Christmas, my brother!" shouted Grand-brother. "We will celebrate, but don't forget your mission. The Golden Star will not remain there for long. Go for it!"

Steve ran and hugged his beloved Christmas tree. He climbed up with Cheeka right behind him. It was a huge tree and climbing it was not easy. Time was passing fast and both boys climbed as fast as they could. They were halfway up the tree when a huge tremor stopped their progress. Steve held on tightly to a branch, while Cheeka clung to the trunk.

The tremor was growing and the boys could hear a huge commotion at a distance. Cheeka sniffed the air and appeared very worried. The tremor and noise grew louder. Then Steve spotted the source: running toward the Forbidden Circle, from all directions, were hundreds of Yetis. They advanced with war cries, all set to grab the Golden Star.

"Cheeka—"

Before Steve could complete his sentence, Cheeka interjected, "I know, I know. I recognized their scent from a distance. If they reach this tree, we're done for!"

Once again Steve had underestimated Grand-brother's foresight and the Viola tribe's commitment to the mission. Grand-brother and his brave warriors were communicating with each other in their sign language. Grand-brother made a violet symbol in the air, and in no time all the ice warriors turned into globules and merged into the snow. The Yetis kept running blindly toward the tree, unaware of what was awaiting them. They ran into the circle and rushed toward the Christmas tree. Once they were all inside the circle, Grand-brother made a signal, and all the ice soldiers sprang up from the snow and pulled the net of ice strings. The very next moment, all the Yetis were down on the ground. The ice strings that appeared thin were so strong that not one of those humungous creatures could move.

"Brother Steve! You are safe. Go on!" shouted Grand-brother. Tired as they were, Steve and Cheeka continued their progress up the tree. But they had lost a lot of time, and, to their great desperation, the Christmas tree had started its journey back into the earth. Their hands started slipping from the branches. Steve knew that if he lost his grip and fell on the ground, all will be lost.

"Don't give up, my friends!" shouted Grand-brother. "This is your last chance!"

The boys pushed on and were about the reach the Golden Star when a tremendous noise shook the whole mountain range.

"H-a-a-a-a!" shouted King Yeti as he attacked.

The booming yell gave Cheeka such a jolt that he lost his grip and fell. In the nick of time, Steve extended his leg and Cheeka managed to catch it. Steve was shaken up, but somehow managed to hold on, as the Christmas tree gradually moved downward. Steve knew this was his last chance. A little slip and he would not only miss the Golden Star, but would also perish inside the Forbidden Circle.

"Hold on, Cheeka, and don't panic!" said Steve, pulling himself up. He was just about a yard away from the star when King Yeti made a mighty leap from outside the Forbidden Circle, crossing over the nets and landing right on the Christmas tree.

Grand-brother and all his soldiers watched in shock as the Yeti shook the Christmas tree with all his vengeance. Steve and Cheeka were tossed around like tennis balls and barely managed to hang on. Steve pulled himself up, against all odds, and finally got his hand on the Golden Star! But the star was big and he had to hold it with both his hands. With one hand holding a branch, the other hand on the star, and Cheeka hanging on to his leg, Steve felt like he was fighting a losing battle.

The mighty King Yeti used all his strength and shook the Christmas tree violently. Steve could no longer hold on to the branch. He lost his grip and fell. But he did not let go of the Golden Star. Cheeka fell with him. Grand-brother watched him fall and rushed to save him.

As Steve was falling, he heard that almost-forgotten,

wondrous voice, a voice right from the pages of fairy tale books….. "Ho – Ho – Ho – Ho!"

It was Santa Claus, riding his sledge through the air, driven by beautiful reindeer. Santa swiftly came down and caught Steve and Cheeka as they fell from the tree. Steve blinked his eyes in disbelief. Was he dreaming?

"How can this happen?" he thought. Was he really sitting on Santa's lap? He looked at his hands and saw that the Golden Star was with him. He further tightened his grip on it, as the reindeer took off. Not wanting to give up, King Yeti leaped up toward the sled. But it was already beyond his reach, and he fell down into the Forbidden Circle.

As the Golden Star left it, the Forbidden Circle returned to its original state. The gravitational power increased and the Christmas tree went back into the earth. The yetis were also getting pulled in. They struggled, but in vain, because the Violas' net arrested them completely. They had to yield to the power of gravity. Their king, however, had sensed the danger earlier. As the power of gravity increased, he took a giant leap out of the circle. Another few leaps and King Yeti disappeared into the mountains.

Within the next few moments, all the Yetis, the strings, and everything that was present inside the Forbidden Circle disappeared. The place was desolate and deserted once again.

Grand-brother stood silently with his Viola warriors. He looked up at the sky. The moon and the stars had gone back to their original positions. A sense of calm pervaded the atmosphere. He closed his eyes and said, "Thank you, my Lord. Take care of the kids." He stood there in silent meditation, feeling the quietness of the place.

But the silence was broken by the pleasing sound of jingling bells. He opened his eyes and saw the reindeer carrying Santa's sled down toward him.

"Hey, Grand-brother, we missed you!" said Pinkoo, as the sledge came down. Steve and Cheeka also appeared jubilant.

"I missed you too, little one!" said Grand-brother.

"Without your help, we would have never reached the Golden Star," said Cheeka, filled with gratitude.

"We can't thank you enough, Grand-brother." Said Steve, hugging him.

"Our whole Viola tribe joins me to express our deep gratitude to God, for taking great care of you," said Grand-brother, smiling. "Always remember, Gratitude is the simplest and easiest way to get everything you want, my brother. We often forget to thank God for simple things that really don't matter in our everyday life. If we thank him at all, it's when we get something we desire, or something works out the way we want. If things go wrong, we start blaming the same God who is always taking care of us. Have you noticed that the moment we start cribbing for something going wrong, other things also start to spoil? So remember, as long as we complain, we keep getting more reasons to complain. But if we can remain in gratitude, God will keep giving us more and more reasons to be thankful about." The three friends listened to Grand-brother with attention. Santa patted Steve's back and smilingly said, "See, how easy life can be? Just practice gratitude. Say 'Thank You' always."

"We shall remember all that you have said and all that you have done, Grand-brother," said Steve with deep gratitude. "The only thing is…that we don't want to leave you."

"Ha, Ha," laughed Grand-brother, moist eyed. "This is just the beginning," he said, his blue, jewel-like eyes twinkling at Steve. "There is still a long way to go. You have to search and find all seven sacred paintings. I cannot help you with those missions, though. My duty lies with this land…As for now…you could not be in a better company. Santa Clause is your guide. May God and our grandmaster always be with you! So long!"

Grand-brother and all his wonderful ice warriors bid them goodbye as Steve, Cheeka, and Pinkoo rode away in Santa's sled, jingling the bells across the sky, and leaving behind a trail of twinkling rainbow stars. The valley of the Golden Star reverberated with the merriest of pleasing sounds…

"Ho – Ho – Ho – Ho!"
"Ho – Ho – Ho – Ho!"

Steve, Cheeka and Pinkoo move on with their mission…

CPSIA information can be obtained at www.ICGtesting.com
Printed in the USA
LVOW05s1728101014

408235LV00017B/1053/P